# THE NIGHT THEY MURDERED CHELSEA

Chelsea Fortune had to be eliminated. They were all agreed on that. She was no longer just a liability—she had become a threat. And with her reputation it was a wonder she hadn't been murdered long ago. Even so, when the news was leaked to the Press that producer and scriptwriters were planning a gruesome end for one of the major figures in the long-running TV serial *Wild Fortune*, no one could have guessed that on the night they murdered Chelsea, Dame Charlotte Saint-Clair, who played her, would be found murdered in her Sussex home in a manner that precisely paralleled her death on the TV screen.

# THE NIGHT THEY THEY MURDERED CHELSEA

## Margaret Hinxman

*A Lythway Book*

CHIVERS PRESS
BATH

First published 1984
by
William Collins Sons & Co Ltd
This Large Print edition published by
Chivers Press
by arrangement with
William Collins Sons & Co Ltd
and in the U.S.A. with
Dodd, Mead & Co
1985

ISBN 0 7451 0206 9

**British Library Cataloguing in Publication Data**

Hinxman, Margaret
  The night they murdered Chelsea.—Large
  print ed.
  —(A Lythway book)
  I. Title
  823'.914 [F]      PR6058.I5/

  ISBN 0–7451–0206–9

# CHAPTER ONE

The rays of a wintry sun sneaked timidly down past the tall office blocks and department stores of Regent Street, momentarily warming the hordes of shoppers on the pavement below. In a bad year for business the sales had stretched into early February and the feeble breath of approaching spring had brought out the bargain-hunters.

From the top floor of a massively imposing building, which dwarfed the flagship of a famous chain store on one side and a fast food emporium on the other, they seemed like tiny Lowry figures, with spindly legs, hunched bodies, concentrating on surviving the moment, unattached to each other.

'All human life is there,' the girl in the spacious office on the tenth floor murmured tritely, staring out of the window. The double glazing muffled the noise of the traffic and people from the street below, giving the scene the eerie fascination of a disjointedly choreographed ballet from which the music had been curiously omitted.

The three men disregarded her comment, oblivious of what was going on outside until the sun, low in the sky, penetrated the window-pane, sending a shaft of bright light into the

1

smoky room.

Ackerman squinted. 'The blind, Liz.'

She stared at him glumly.

'Only because you're nearest,' he said irritably. She shrugged and pulled down the blind half-way, blocking out the unwelcome sunlight.

Sam Ackerman settled back in his chair behind the cluttered desk which matched his awkward, cluttered appearance: rumpled trousers, shapeless pullover and a none too clean shirt collar untidily circling his thick neck.

'Then it's settled. We've got to get rid of her.' His voice was toneless as if he were reiterating a decision that had already been established many times.

'Absolutely.' The new voice, by contrast, was soft, pliant, lacking authority. It was a voice to which habitual agreement came naturally. Mack Tully crossed one thin grey-flannelled leg neatly over the other and nervously fingered his already impeccably tied tie. He sat on the edge of his chair facing Ackerman. Waiting.

Three pairs of eyes—Ackerman's shrewd, cold; Tully's anxious, questioning; Liz Briley's thoughtful, amused—focused on the third man.

'Why keep stating the obvious? We've no choice. She's forced our hand. Chelsea Fortune has to be eliminated.' John Arthur smiled, studying the doodle he'd been making on a foolscap pad: a matchstick sketch of a woman

2

with wild, curly hair, no features and a long chain round her neck.

'The bitch has got to go. She's no longer just a liability, she's a threat—to everyone.'

'We know that,' Ackerman said grimly. He picked up his coffee cup, drained it and flicked a glance at the empty percolator on the side table. 'The question . . .'

'The question is, how do we polish her off?' Arthur continued.

'As quietly and discreetly as possible,' volunteered Tully, quickly, as if surprised at his own daring. Ackerman shook his head.

'That *would* be your solution. Quiet, discreet. Shut up, Mack, and make us some more coffee.'

'I could do with something stronger,' said Liz Briley.

'You can do without it.' They all knew when Ackerman meant business.

'Make it look like an accident,' she said briskly, then seemed to change her mind. 'My God, it's gruesome, spending three hours plotting the death of a woman. A human being.' She shuddered.

'I didn't know you were so squeamish, Liz.'

He swivelled his chair round as if avoiding the accusing gaze of the beautiful, proud, patrician woman in the photograph on the desk, with its silver filigree frame and flowery inscription: 'To Sam—from your grateful Chelsea.'

'I didn't know you were so callous, *Mr*

3

Ackerman. She has her good points.'

'It's not hard being callous about Chelsea. She deserves all she's going to get.'

John Arthur raised his slender hands over his head and brought them smartly together. 'Don't let's start fighting among ourselves. That's fatal.'

'You're right,' growled Ackerman. 'We're here to discuss a more important fatality—and three bloody hours we've been at it!'

'Perhaps—perhaps we could get George to slip her an overdose.'

'George! George hasn't the guts to slip an extra spoonful of sugar in her tea,' Mack Tully muttered as he plugged in the percolator.

Ackerman nodded. 'For once I agree with Mack. George would never have the nerve, although, heaven knows, he has good cause to see her dead.'

'I still think it should look like an accident; less aggro with the police,' Liz repeated.

'Too many slip-ups with an accident.' John Arthur indicated quotes round the word 'accident' with his forefingers. 'It should be a very clear case of murder.'

It was the first time any of them had actually mentioned murder although it had been on their minds all morning. The thought silenced the four conspirators. Ackerman, as usual, spoke first.

'Easier said than done.'

'Easily said, easily done,' said Arthur. 'We'll strangle her with that damned gold chain she wears all the time. Perfect. Rough but perfect justice.' He picked up his ballpoint pen and deftly completed his doodle with a thick noose looped round the neck of the matchstick woman.

'It's so, so—heavy,' said Liz. 'The idea, I mean. I shouldn't like . . .'

'You won't have to. The deed will be done by somebody of our choosing.'

Ackerman ran a hand through his thick fuzz of grey hair.

'Nice. Very nice. Tasty. I can just see her when that somebody takes her by surprise. She's got to suffer. She's got to be made to suffer. After all, she's caused enough suffering in her time.'

'I like it.' Mack Tully poured the coffee into dirty cups with a more confident hand.

'Ugh,' said Liz. 'But yes. And the beauty is, there will be so many suspects the police won't know where to start. With her reputation, it's a wonder she hasn't been murdered long ago.'

'Changed your tune? What about her good points?'

'There aren't so many,' Liz admitted.

'Right, then.' Ackerman eased his clumsy bulk out of his chair. 'We've two planning weeks, no longer. We've got the frame, now all we've got to do is fill in the details. Let me have

5

some thoughts in a few days. Meanwhile, we'll go on as if everything is normal. I assume we all trust each other enough not to betray any of this conversation even, or perhaps especially, to our nearest and dearest?'

They all murmured agreement, realizing there was no need. They knew each other too well.

'When?' asked Liz. 'I mean—Chelsea?'

Ackerman thought for a moment, then his heavily lined face creased into a broad, crafty grin. 'April first, of course. April Fool's Day. Neat, don't you think?'

He heaved himself into a shabby suede jacket lined with grimy sheepskin and moved towards the door. He was unexpectedly light on his feet for such a large man.

His eyes scanned the littered room. 'We can leave this for the cleaners. Except for that doodle.' He pointed in the direction of John Arthur's pad. 'I've had it. See you on Monday. But don't waste time. I want results.' He grinned again with relish. 'The final solution.'

'What about me?' said Mack Tully plaintively.

'No problem. When we've finalised the plan, you can do what you think necessary, in all our interests.'

He unlocked the door and they heard him call to his secretary in the office outside. 'I won't be back today, Ivy.'

'What about the messages? You told me to hold the calls.' Her voice sounded exasperated but guarded. Ackerman was a formidable force, not to be challenged lightly.

'They'll keep,' he said over his shoulder as he made purposefully for the lift.

'Well, that's that.' Liz gathered together her belongings, the masculine severity of her anorak, pants and long boots emphasizing the femininity of her figure and immaculately cut straw-coloured hair which framed a deceptively youthful face.

'Thank the Lord, that's over,' sighed Mack Tully.

'Nightmares, Mack?' drawled Liz.

'Wouldn't know I was asleep if I didn't have a nightmare.'

John Arthur chuckled quietly. 'We, old sport, are about to embark on a nightmare that will make all other nightmares seem like a moonlight frolic with E.T.'

Liz shuddered again. 'Poor, rich old Chelsea.'

'First time you've ever expressed sympathy for Chelsea Fortune. You hate her guts. Second thoughts?'

'No.' She shook her head.

'Poor, rich, dead old Chelsea!' A dark shadow smudged the sharp outlines of the face in the photograph on the desk, accentuating those accusing eyes. They seemed to stare back at John Arthur, watchful, aware, alive. But it was

7

only a trick of the light.

The three of them left the office and braced themselves to join the unknowing crowds in Regent Street. The sun had long since given up the unequal struggle to pierce the clouds, which now hovered greyly over the busy London thoroughfare.

*     *     *

Two weeks later Mack Tully telephoned the show business correspondent of the Fleet Street tabloid with the largest circulation, the *Daily Globe*. They arranged to meet at a favourite pub. The next day a breathless item was heavily featured as an exclusive on the 'What's New In TV' page.

It's shock horror time for the millions of fans worldwide of the phenomenally successful TV series *'Wild Fortune.'* Regent TV publicist Mack Tully tells me that producer Samuel Ackerman and writers Liz Briley and John Arthur are planning a gruesome end for the much-loathed matriarch, Chelsea Fortune, of the doom-laden Fortune family.

It's been an open secret that the fine actress Dame Charlotte Saint-Clair who plays her has been wanting out of the series for a long time. But she couldn't have guessed how spectacularly she will be ousted. For further news—Watch This Space.

## CHAPTER TWO

The newsflash leaked to the *Globe* had precisely the desired effect planned by Sam Ackerman and Mack Tully. It created an excitement that would certainly gather momentum until the day on April 1st when the last fateful episode of the current season of *Wild Fortune* was to be transmitted on television. It was a calculated exercise in mass media suspense.

There had been nothing like it since the 'Who Shot J.R.?' cliff-hanger in *Dallas*. The campaign had been plotted in exact detail. The leak. The public speculation. The follow-through with shrewdly planted features in newspapers, magazines and even on TV itself. Ackerman realized how fruitful the meeting in his office on that February morning had been when *News At Ten* noted the interest aroused by the prospect of Chelsea Fortune's departure from the series as a footnote to sterner news. True, they'd made a joke of it. But then it was a joke. That, thought Ackerman with smug satisfaction, is entertainment.

Even he, an old hand in movies and

television, had been surprised at the instant audience response to *Wild Fortune*. He'd envisaged it running for a season, maybe two. But it had topped the TV ratings now for five years and showed no signs of loosening its grip on the public's imagination. Sales abroad had ensured that the dire dramas of the Fortune family, the in-fighting of its members, their double dealings in very big business and the evil manipulations of the linch-pin of the series, Chelsea, were as avidly watched in America, Europe and Australia as they were in Britain. Fan clubs swore allegiance to one character or another. Acres of newsprint were devoted to fleshing out their lives, speculating on their background, building on the framework laid down by the head writers Liz Briley and John Arthur.

When reporters asked Ackerman to explain its popularity, he solemnly trotted out clichés about well-researched plots, believable characters, an extraordinarily well-chosen cast and, of course, the driving force of Charlotte Saint-Clair. 'With an actress like her playing Chelsea, how could we lose?' he'd say, and the reporters would sagely agree.

But he knew that was just an excuse for an answer. It was a competently made formula series which, for some indefinable reasons, had clicked beyond anyone's wildest hopes. Not for the first time he was reminded that the TV audience out there—those faceless millions of people who could create, retard or destroy careers with the flick of a knob—was a totally unpredictable animal. He'd made better films, produced better TV series and, while he relished the fruits of the success of *Wild Fortune,* a secret part of him resented it. If he were remembered at all, it would be as the producer of a TV freak.

When, in December, Charlotte Saint-Clair had delivered her ultimatum that she didn't wish to renew her contract for the next series of *Wild Fortune,* it had seemed at first a shattering blow: even though Sam, Mack, Liz, John, who had lived with it since its inception, reassured each other that the series was bigger than one single character.

Apart from the legal department of the TV company, they'd kept it to themselves. The journeymen directors, who each did a batch of three or four episodes, and the rest of the cast didn't need to be told yet and Charlotte had agreed. 'Just write me out with style,' she'd stipulated gaily.

It was only later, when they'd had time to assess the situation which confronted them, that they'd appreciated the publicity capital that could be made out of eliminating Chelsea. 'Interest in the series must flag,' Mack had pointed out. 'It has to. It's the law of averages. This could give it a fantastic boost. It could go on forever.'

Inwardly Ackerman groaned. Forever! But Mack had made sense in his usual frenetic way.

'Only if you keep them guessing,' Liz had observed in that low, agreeable voice which had charmed many a producer into believing she couldn't possibly be as tough as her reputation. 'And not just the public and the press. The cast, too—and Chelsea. No one but us should know exactly what's going to happen to her practically until the day we film the episode when she leaves.'

'Charlotte won't like that.' John Arthur had been scratching away with his ballpoint on the pad that was as much a part of him as his ridiculous Mickey Mouse wristwatch and bizarre gold signet ring which always seemed too weighty for his delicate hand.

'Charlotte is hardly in a position to object,' said Ackerman. 'After all, she got us into this situation.'

He remembered that conversation as he sat in Charlotte's small, elegant London flat just off Kensington High Street the day after the item appeared in the *Daily Globe*.

★    ★    ★

'She won't be a minute. The *masseuse* is with her.' Joanna Saint-Clair efficiently placed a tray of coffee on the fragile inlaid rosewood table at his elbow. Before he could thank her, she'd settled herself at the small desk by the window, where she busied herself opening the pile of letters on the blotting-pad. She'd always made it plain that she didn't like Ackerman, not in so many words, but in the deft way she managed to avoid undue contact with him.

He could never understand why she didn't like him. He quite liked her. In fact he'd felt rather sorry for the reserved girl constantly living in the shadow of the famous, glamorous aunt who made what seemed to him impossible demands on her time, blood-ties and capable qualities as companion-secretary. He'd even found himself speculating on what a decent hairdresser and cosmetic artist could do for her. Working as he did with actresses adept at making the most of what God had given them, he couldn't understand why any young woman should deliberately play down her best features.

She could never be the raving beauty her aunt had been and still was in her seventies, but she had interesting, rather severe features, arresting brown eyes when they weren't masked behind owlish spectacles and a figure that probably wasn't bad if it weren't invariably encased in a severely tailored tweed suit. Fashion seemed to have passed Joanna Saint-Clair by, along with youth and carefree pleasure.

The silence between them was uncomfortable.

'Mail never stops,' he said idly, stupidly. It seemed more appropriate than commenting on the weather.

'What would you expect—after yesterday.' Her tone didn't invite a reply.

Come *on*, Charlie, he thought. After all, you invited me.

He studied the room as he had many times before, struck as always by how indelibly Charlotte had stamped her personality on it. There was, of course, the gallery of photographs—Charlotte with Noel, Charlotte with Fred and Ginger, Charlotte with Gable, Charlotte with Louis B. Mayer and an eager young Judy Garland, Charlotte with Leila Starr. All effusively inscribed. There was the obligatory portrait of her in her Hollywood heyday hanging over the mantelpiece, painted by an indifferent artist, although his meagre talent couldn't disguise the luminous quality of the subject.

But it was more than just the theatrical extravagance of the flat that made it so personally Charlotte Saint-Clair's. It was the refinement of the decor; the perfect toning of colours in carpets, curtains and furnishings; the delicate antique pieces that had been chosen not as an investment but with the impeccable taste of a woman who cherished the feel of fine wood, silver and china; the pictures and bric-à-brac collected over years of travelling the world

14

which hadn't been devalued by time. All had their place. Even the garish portrait didn't seem at odds with the tiny Picasso spotlighted in the alcove in the corner of the room.

He stood up awkwardly—he never could seem to contain his bulk—and walked across to the alcove. Like Charlotte, the Picasso glowed with its own inner strength. Amazing what a genius could do with a few exact brush strokes, he thought.

'One of these days, Sam, I believe you'll murder me for that Picasso.'

She'd entered the room silently and was standing behind him. But he felt her presence, overpowering, diminishing everything and everybody within eye range of her. It was her special quality, the reason why the camera had fallen in love with her during her years as a Hollywood star; the reason why audiences were still captivated by her, persuading themselves that the years had made no inroads on that astonishing face.

'Charlie!' He turned and brushed her cheek perfunctorily with his lips. The traditional show business greeting. 'You look wonderful.' The traditional show business salute. Except that Ackerman meant it. She did look wonderful.

Apart from a smudge of mascara she wore no make-up, her face pink and gleaming after the ministrations of skilful fingers. The headband she wore to protect her unashamedly white hair

15

made a striking frame for those classic features, the high skeletal cheekbones, the Roman nose, the powerful jawline, the chameleon eyes that could be stormy when she was angered and softly enticing when she was pleased.

She held herself erectly, a floating rainbow-flecked housecoat expertly disguising breasts that were now sagging, a thickened waist, flesh which—despite the efforts of the *masseuse*—had long since lost the sap of youth. But if age had defiled the texture of the body, it couldn't destroy its grace.

Charlotte didn't move, she floated; only the walking stick in her hand betrayed the signs of rheumatism with which she was plagued. And she even used the walking stick more as a stage prop than a physical necessity, Ackerman thought admiringly.

'Amazing what a good *masseuse* can do with an old gel, isn't it?' she said lightly, deriding the term 'old gel' for the patent mockery it was. The fluting voice could still imbue the most trivial remark with the resonance she'd once brought to Shakespeare, Shaw, Ibsen and Chekhov.

He marvelled that after all these years she could still exercise the same spell over him that she had when he'd first glimpsed her when he was a humble clapper-boy at Pinewood Studios thirty years before.

'So let's get down to business, Sam.' He recognized and respected the tone of steel that

16

cut through the formalities. 'What's this I read in that—that rag? What does it say, Joanna?' She flicked a glance across her shoulder at the hunched figure of the young woman opening envelopes at the desk.

'"Producer Samuel Ackerman," etcetera, etcetera, "planning a gruesome end for the much-loathed matriarch, Chelsea Fortune," etcetera, etcetera, "spectacularly ousted".' As Joanna Saint-Clair quoted the item in the *Daily Globe* in a dry monotone, the words taken out of context seemed even more absurd than they appeared in print.

'Well, Sam?' Charlotte settled herself in a high commanding chair, arranged her housecoat becomingly and fixed her eyes—decidedly stormy—on him. Her fingers fiddled restlessly with the long, heavy gold chain she habitually wore around her neck. Ackerman occasionally wondered if she wore it in bed. But as he'd never been there, to his eternal regret, he could only speculate.

Sam smiled, his accommodating smile, he hoped.

'My dear Charlie. It's just a publicity ploy. You know the business. When the most important character in the highest rated series on television disappears from it, naturally there's going to be a lot of interest. Interest? Furore! My phone hasn't stopped ringing this morning.'

'Sam, you're avoiding the issue. I'm not questioning the interest. I'm enough of a pro to be bothered if there weren't any interest. I'm just wondering what you and Liz and John have cooked up between you as a fitting end for me. If it's anything like rape and mugging, I'll . . .'

'Calm down, Charlie. Of course it's nothing like that. And you can wheedle as much as you like but you're not going to know what's to happen until you get the script,' he added.

'I think I should have been consulted.' She paused. 'So does Joanna.'

It was, Ackerman judged, the moment to be firm. 'Charlie, it was *your* decision to leave the series. We didn't want you to go. And I don't recall anything in your contract which specifically requires script approval, except in general character terms.'

Charlotte studied her long, bony fingers intently.

Finally she said, 'You're quite right, legally. But for the sake of friendship. What . . . what exactly does "gruesome" mean? I have to think of my reputation.'

'OK. I'll tell you this much. Chelsea is going to be murdered.'

He waited anxiously for her reaction. Unexpectedly, he noted a slight smile hovering around the corner of her lips.

'Murdered spectacularly,' she murmured as if testing the idea and finding it palatable.

Ackerman quickly capitalized on her mellowing attitude towards Chelsea's end. Charlotte's opposition would make no difference, but an angry actress—particularly such a celebrated one as Charlotte—could make herself a formidable nuisance during the filming of the episode.

'Look at it this way. Because of you, your talent, your personality, your charisma'—he was piling it on thick but he didn't care—'Chelsea Fortune has become the most famous character on television.

'Half the public adores her for doing all the ruthless things they'd like to do but wouldn't dare. The other half loathes her for the same reason. You can't just slip out of the series, take a long trip to Australia and never come back. That would be a ticket to oblivion. This way you go out with real—' he searched for the right word and found it—'with real *panache*. Horrible, of course. Murder is horrible. But how else would Chelsea want to go? Even in death she'll be sure of making an almighty stir.'

As he gave her a moment to digest what he'd said, he was struck again at how even the people who invented these fictional characters talked about them as if they had a genuine flesh and blood life, as if they were more real than the performers who portrayed them. If he and Charlotte and Liz and John couldn't differentiate between fact and fantasy, what

19

chance did the viewing public have?

She nodded, twirling the chain round and round in that irritating habit of hers. 'I can see that. But why the secrecy?'

'Because, dear Charlie, the longer we keep it secret, the more avid everyone will be to watch that episode. The ratings will go right through the ceiling. It will empty every pub, cinema and theatre in the country. The name of Chelsea Fortune will be on everyone's lips.'

'And what about my name? I've got one too.'

'No one could ever forget it, Charlie. It wasn't created by Chelsea. You're not some novice actress who'd never had a career before she appeared on television. You're an institution. Your family—Saint-Clair—is part of Britain's theatrical history. Every other night they show one of your old movies on the box and you make a million more fans.'

Suddenly the luminous eyes became grave. 'Sam,' she said quietly, 'do *you* think I'm loathed—like Chelsea?'

The question, so unexpected, startled Sam. Much more startling, she seemed to need an answer.

# CHAPTER THREE

Joanna Saint-Clair looked up abruptly from the mail she'd been reading. Apart from reciting the contents of the item in the *Globe*, she'd seemed not to be aware of the conversation to-ing and fro-ing behind her back.

'Aunt Charlotte, what a ridiculous thing to say. How could you possibly even imagine that you were anything like that—that creature on television.'

Ackerman flashed her a thankful smile for having taken the edge off a sticky moment. She puckered her lips and lowered her eyes, but he felt for the first time they were in accord. His relationship with Charlotte had been professional, businesslike when they were doing the job, superficial when they met socially.

She never brought her troubles to him as the rest of the regular cast did incessantly. He'd never had to smooth over crises for her or cope with sudden displays of temperament. That was part of the joy of working with her.

That she should hint at the concern she'd expressed suggested a lowering of defences that made him feel embarrassed.

'Joanna's right, Charlie. It's a ridiculous thought. You're the best-loved actress I know. And you know it too,' he chided her. 'You're just fishing.'

'Am I? Perhaps you don't know me so well, Sam. You don't get to be a success without trampling a few people underfoot on the way up.'

He conceded the truth of that. 'It's the nature of the profession.'

'Have I ever told you, Sam, how grateful I am to you? Perhaps I should—before it's too late.' She corrected herself. 'Before I leave the series.'

'Don't I have that photograph of you on my desk: "To Sam—from your grateful Chelsea"? In the silver frame you bought in the flea market in Paris. You see, I remember everything.'

She chuckled, the lovely, gurgling chuckle that had charmed Cary Grant and Spencer Tracy and Melvyn Douglas and all her other leading men.

'That was Chelsea. This is from me. You know when you asked me to do the series that my career, as they say, was on the skids. I'd used up my time. Hollywood had changed. I'd played all the great roles I wanted to play at the Old Vic and Royal Shakespeare. There was virtually no British film industry. I was wealthy and unemployed. Between engagements. But you wanted me.'

'It had been a dream of mine since I saw you on the set at Pinewood in the nineteen-fifties. You didn't notice me. A clapper-boy. But I knew you.'

22

'That dreadful film! *Love in Exile*. Bette and Joan and Vivien had all turned it down. But that ghastly man, what was his name, Lou Hacker, didn't tell me that. We all knew it was a turkey. Although I understand it's considered quite a cult movie now. The young *cinéastes* are discovering great, profound depths in it. It's very nice of them, but quite untrue. The script was just cobbled together as we went along. Did you know they're going to run a retrospective of my films at the National Film Theatre?'

He didn't. But he was glad that the thought seemed to cheer her up enormously.

'I confess I'll be glad to get rid of Chelsea. She started to invade my life in a way I'd never experienced before. I was never one for taking a role home with me. Like Noel and Larry, I learned the lines, did the job and then packed it neatly away with the costumes and scenery. I don't think I'd identified with a character since I played Juliet as a young girl at the Birmingham Rep. I fell madly in love with Romeo and contemplated suicide briefly when he married the assistant stage manager. The next day the European talent scout for M-G-M called me up and I forgot all about Romeo. Can't even remember his name.'

'What will you do, Charlie, when you leave the show?'

'First a long rest. I haven't visited the cottage in Sussex for months. Then—who knows?'

'You'll be very hot. What about the theatre?'

'I couldn't carry the lines any more, Sam. There—that's an admission. Age. To tell you the truth, lately I've even found the series taxing. When you're seventy your memory plays tricks.'

He grinned inwardly. He knew for a fact that she was at least seventy-three. He didn't know an actress who hadn't publicly shed a few years as her career progressed.

'No, Sam, what I'd like is a nice juicy cameo role in a hugely expensive film which will win me an Oscar. I'd rather enjoy standing up there again thanking all the people I'd been battling with during the production, and being kissed on the cheek by Paul Newman or Dustin Hoffman who would then make a nice little speech about my services to the industry.'

He looked at his watch. Reminiscences were pleasant, but time was pressing.

'We'd appreciate it if you could make yourself available for interviews. Nothing too taxing, although I'm pretty sure the heavies might want to photograph you at the cottage in Sussex. Mack Tully has a schedule worked out.'

She screwed up her regal nose in an expression of faint distaste. 'Uncouth man, Tully.'

'Mack! Uncouth! I'd always thought him rather natty. I'm the uncouth one.'

'To other people maybe. Not to me, Sam.

Never to me. Very well, a few well-chosen interviews, if it would help the series.'

'And then after the show—a wonderful retirement. I envy you.'

'Not so much of the retirement. Like old soldiers, old actresses never die, they simply fade away.' Her voice seemed to float away into the middle distance, a trick she'd employed so successfully on stage. 'I wonder. I wonder.'

She pulled her thoughts together and briskly motioned to her niece. 'It's time we got down to those letters, Joanna. Very touching, some of them. I'm sorry, Sam, I didn't even offer you a drink.'

'Never before midday.'

'And not much after. You're very abstemious, I've noticed.'

At this stage he wasn't about to embark on the story of his problems with alcoholism which he had painfully licked ten years ago.

He heard Joanna rustling papers in that purposeful manner which indicated his time was up.

'I'll see you at the run-through tomorrow then, Charlie. And I'll tell Mack you agree to the interviews?'

She sighed. 'Happily it's a light episode for me. What is it? Off to Washington to confer with some senator about a transatlantic financial fiddle. Out of sight . . .'

'But not out of mind.' Sam completed the

cliché.

'What a giggle it all is! Romeo, Romeo, wherefore art thou Romeo?'

Sam smiled. 'Probably running a pub in Bridlington with the former assistant stage manager behind the bar.'

'Or dead.'

He thought he detected the suspicion of a tear in her eye. Maybe she hadn't entirely forgotten that Romeo from Birmingham Rep.

★    ★    ★

When he returned to the offices of Regent TV he learned that the phones had been ringing all morning. The 'end of Chelsea' episode wouldn't be recorded for a fortnight, several weeks before transmission, but everyone in Fleet Street, it seemed, was trying to call in favours, begging for a scoop, a hint of how Sam was going to dispose of Chelsea Fortune.

'It's been chaos around here,' his secretary Ivy informed him darkly.

'That's what you're paid for, coping with chaos,' Sam said curtly, reverting back to his old bearish image.

Without knocking he barged into the office shared by Liz Briley and John Arthur and the freelance writers who contributed to the series. If anything, it looked more of a mess than it usually did: ashtrays overflowing with cigarette butts, a regiment of mugs half filled with cold black coffee, wastepaper baskets spilling out their contents on the green cord-carpeted floor. On the wall the chart that detailed the genealogy and transgressions of the Fortune Family since that fractious mob first hit the TV screens was a maze of scribbled emendations and alterations, indecipherable to anyone who hadn't lived with the series from its birth.

Liz was visibly holding in her impatience as she talked to some persistant caller on the telephone.

'I know ... I know ... Bert ... I appreciate ... But ...' She cupped her hand over the receiver and raised weary eyebrows. 'Can't get a word in edgewise,' she whispered to Sam, then into the mouthpiece firmly: 'Look, Bert, there's nothing I can do. No information. Production edict. I know you've always been a love. I know you gave us our first break in the Press. But this is bigger that both of us. You'll have to take it up with Sam Ackerman.'

Ackerman shook his head.

'But you can't get him today,' Liz took the hint, 'Sorry, Bert, I have to go now—the other phone's ringing.'

She put down the receiver abruptly and slumped back in her chair, her skirt fetchingly revealing a length of slim thigh.

'Whew! I wish to God we could tell the world that Chelsea Fortune is going to be strangled with her own gold chain. Then maybe we'd get a bit of peace to do the job.'

John Arthur chuckled. They were a good team. He relaxed, reasonable. She quick-tempered, high on inspiration.

'You know you love it. All the fuss. Superstar Television writer,' he said.

'Sod you, genius,' she replied fondly.

'How'd it go with Charlotte?'

Ackerman stole a cigarette from the pack at John Arthur's elbow.

'Surprisingly well. Good old girl, she's a pro. She liked the idea of going out with a bang. Even agreed to cooperate with Mack about the publicity angle.'

'You didn't tell her how she was going to be murdered?'

'No. Just that it wouldn't be anything filthy like rape and mugging. Anyway, it'll be a great end for this series and it'll give us plenty of scope for the next one.'

John Arthur made a face as he swallowed some cold coffee. 'I still think George is the best one.'

They'd worked together so long they hardly needed to communicate in words, catching the threads of each other's thoughts before they were expressed. 'George' was Chelsea Fortune's weakling son-in-law and one of many candidates for her murderer under consideration.

'No one would believe it.' Ackerman had

28

scant regard for the actor, Baxter Hadley, who played him. Liz and John exchanged knowing glances.

'What you really mean is you don't want to hand Bax a bonus of fruity scenes in which he's apprehended, interrogated and brought to trial,' said Liz. 'The public will believe it because it *is* unbelievable. Surprise, surprise, dopey George getting up the nerve to commit murder!'

She could see that Ackerman's professionalism was making inroads on his prejudice. 'We'll see,' he agreed. 'But we don't have to decide that now. We've enough on our plate, getting this series out of the way.'

'Well, all the location shooting's been done, so it should be plain sailing in the studio.' John Arthur could be trusted to look on the bright side.

'If only the Press would get off our backs,' said Liz gloomily.

'How's Mack holding up?'

'Just barely, but you know Mack. He thrives on crises, even though he always thinks he's on the verge of a nervous breakdown.'

She wasn't wrong. Mack Tulley had kept his nervous breakdown at bay for more years than he cared to remember. He was a good publicist of the old school, chummy with his drinking buddies of the Press, though constantly nervous of the famous names he had to promote, cajole, comfort. Sometimes, the not so famous names, like Baxter Hadley, were more difficult.

During the following days, he was relieved to see, Charlotte Saint-Clair played her part beautifully, not just in front of the camera but off-set as well.

She posed for press photographs at her cottage in Sussex and graciously allowed herself to be interviewed for television, magazines and newspapers.

For women's magazines she mourned that she'd never been blessed with a child; remembered lovingly her dead husband, a bit-part actor named Christopher Devane with whom she'd spent two stormy years before despatching him to oblivion comforted by a handsome settlement; and radiantly insisted that her ageing years had been transformed when her niece Joanna had come to live with her.

For the tabloids she reeled off anecdotes about her Hollywood years; hinted at love-affairs with celebrated male stars; recalled her deep affection for her friendly rival in so many films, Leila Starr—'now, alas, no longer with us'—and wouldn't be drawn on the subject of Leila's suicide in the 1950s.

For the Sunday 'heavies' she relived her important years in the theatre, after Hollywood, at the Old Vic and Royal Shakespeare: her sense of pride when she heard she'd been named in the Queen's birthday honours in 1970 ('although I've always felt the honour was for the profession rather than for me'); and her sadness that she could no longer contribute to the glory of her first and abiding love, the theatre.

If the other members of the cast of *Wild Fortune* were a trifle piqued at the amount of publicity Charlotte was getting, they wisely kept it to themselves. After all, with Charlotte no longer acting them off the screen their own prospects looked more inviting for the next series.

There was no question that she would be replaced: the next star would rise from the ranks. The *Daily Globe* invited readers to select the character most likely to dominate the new format *Wild Fortune*, *sans* Chelsea.

Its rival ran a competition in which fans speculated on how Chelsea would be written out of the series, the reader who came closest to what happened on the screen would win a new Renault hatchback and a trip to the studio.

Letters continued to pour into Regent TV offices from all over the world, some plaintively begging 'don't kill Chelsea', most damning her to hell, until the staff of secretaries cursed the clown who'd invented Chelsea Fortune.

Sam Ackerman breathed a sigh of relief on the day that copies of the script of the last lethal episode were distributed to the cast and crew. It was practically over. He'd promised himself a couple of weeks sunning himself in the Bahamas and looked forward to the restful prospect with deep pleasure. He was contemplating imaginary deserted beaches and an endless horizon of sparkling ocean when Liz Briley burst angrily into his office.

'What's up?' He saw from the look on her face that whatever was up wasn't going to be agreeable.

'What's up? She won't do it—she bloody well won't do it.'

## CHAPTER FOUR

On the permanent set of the grandiose Fortune family drawing-room at Regent TV studios in Hammersmith, Charlotte Saint-Clair sat stubbornly erect in the stately armchair from which she habitually commanded the shady financial operations that were the lifeblood of *Wild Fortune*.

The cast, assembled for a run-through of the final episode of the current series, maintained an awkward silence as if a misplaced word might touch off an explosion.

'I've never known her like this before.' The director, Lester Ruddy, had worked with Charlotte many times during the run of the series and had been specifically chosen by

Ackerman for this episode because of his amicable relationship with the star. 'You try again,' he urged John Arthur.

'There's no point,' said John. 'She's adamant. Let's wait for Sam. He shouldn't be long. I phoned twenty minutes ago.' He checked the time on his childish Mickey Mouse wristwatch which only seemed to irritate Ruddy more.

'Why don't you get yourself a decent watch?' he said with a venom the remark didn't warrant.

'Suits me. Sentimental value.' John Arthur's unruffled composure was almost as exasperating as Charlotte's intractable refusal to accept the script in its present form.

'So we just hang around and wait.'

'That's right. We hang around and wait. It'll all sort itself out.' John Arthur returned to his inevitable doodling, filling in the anguished features of a corpse in a pool of blood.

Elaine Pelham peeked over his shoulder. 'Don't you ever do pretty doodles?'

'Never. Death concentrates my mind wonderfully.' He grinned cheerfully.

He was on affable terms with all the cast of *Wild Fortune*, even Baxter Hadley. Jane Connor, squat and cuddly, the maiden aunt to whom all the Fortune family took their troubles. Ray Harding, the heart-throb of the 'B' movies whose career had been revitalized when he'd been cast against type as the ruthless son who constantly threatened Chelsea's authority. Faith

33

Turner, the *femme fatale* daughter-in-law whose scandalous sex life spiced the boardroom dramas of the Fortune empire.

But Elaine Pelham was special, an actress whose range and depth made a mockery of the stock character she played: Chelsea's much married formidable daughter who played the empire-building game as effectively as her fictional mother. If Charlotte was the acknowledged star, Elaine's was the personality that gave the series the solidity of conviction. It was she who willed audiences to suspend disbelief. Without perhaps realizing it, they recognized quality.

It was common knowledge that she'd turned down offers of leading roles in the legitimate theatre to stick with *Wild Fortune*. John Arthur had often wondered why. The money was good in television, but she hadn't struck him as an actress who would favour a healthy bank balance above prestige in her profession.

'I like the security,' she'd said more than once, 'and I like being stopped in the street and asked for my autograph.' But her protestations hadn't rung true.

'Can you understand what's bugging Charlie?' she asked him now. 'She's always been the least temperamental actress I know.'

John Arthur shrugged. 'Some bee in her bonnet.'

'I can understand. It's the chain.' He looked

up abruptly from his pad at Jane Connor. She had a sweetly infuriating habit of being right, he'd noticed. Her mind was a jumble of high intelligence and mundane trivia and she seemed incapable of differentiating between the two. Proust and the price of Brussels sprouts were discussed in the same plaintive monotone.

Already she'd forgotten the chain and was admiring Elaine's Marks and Spencer overnight case which she maintained was quite as good as Gucci and such fantastic value.

'What do you mean—about the chain?'

She puckered her rosy, round face trying to recall the significance she'd attached to Charlotte's chain. 'Oh yes. The chain. Well, I wouldn't want to be strangled with my own chain, would you?' Then, barely without pausing, she launched into a long dissertation about a nasty experience she'd had shopping in Rome which was somehow connected with Marks and Spencer and Gucci.

'I suppose it could be,' said Elaine over Jane's placid babbling.

Before John Arthur could answer, Sam Ackerman stormed into the studio, closely followed by Liz Briley who hadn't enjoyed the uncomfortable drive they'd shared to Hammersmith.

'What the hell's going on?' he bellowed angrily to no one in particular, fastidiously averting his eyes from the ashen-faced

Charlotte.

Lester Ruddy sighed. 'She read the script and said she wouldn't do it. You'll have to talk her round, Sam. I thought it was all agreed. No problems. We haven't got forever.'

'Too right we haven't.'

They watched silently as he approached the throne upon which Charlotte was seated. He drew up a stool, crouched clumsily at her feet and took her hand in his. Their conversation was conducted in whispers; Sam conciliatory, sympathetic; Charlotte, at first firm, implacable, then tearful, pleading.

The embarrassing sight of the majestic actress reduced to tears was one none of them relished. 'Can't someone rustle up some coffee?' Lester said gruffly, switching the focus of attention. It was the cue they needed to busy themselves with anything rather than concentrate on the two figures absorbed in urgent discussion in the centre of the set.

After what seemed like hours but was probably only a few minutes, Sam Ackerman stood up and walked over to John Arthur and Lester Ruddy.

'You'll just have to come up with something. She won't—I mean she won't let Chelsea be strangled with her chain.'

So, thought John, Jane *had* been right.

'What's wrong with it? Surely she can see it's so much part of the character, she wears it in every scene, there'd be a nice irony in her being murdered with it. And anyway, why couldn't she tell me that?' said Ruddy. Actresses! You thought you knew them, then you discovered you didn't know them at all.

'It's personal.'

'What do you mean—*personal*? For Christ's sake, it's just a TV series!'

'She doesn't want Chelsea, the character, killed with her own gold chain.'

'I know that. You don't have to draw a diagram.'

'You don't get the point, Les,' John interjected quietly. 'It's Charlotte's chain, not Chelsea's. Isn't that it, Sam?'

'That's it.'

'Then there's no problem. We'll get another chain just like it and use that. It shouldn't be difficult to find one that's similar enough to fool the camera. It's not all that special.'

For the first time that morning the anxiety seemed to drain out of Lester Ruddy's face.

'Would she go for that, Sam?'

Ackerman nodded. 'I think she'll buy it.'

In the event it took another half-hour's hard talking to persuade Charlotte to accept the compromise. Reluctantly she allowed the wardrobe mistress, whom she trusted, to take the chain to the nearest jeweller's to match it.

It was the first time Ackerman had seen it in the hand instead of elegantly wound round

Charlotte's neck.

It was a heavy Victorian piece made up of interlocking double gold rings. There was nothing particularly distinctive about it. There were thousands of imitation costume jewellery chains almost indistinguishable from it in the department stores and boutiques. Only the clasp was unique: two linking letters picked out in tiny amethysts, the traditional mourning stones of the Victorians which replaced the widow's jet after the immediate period of bereavement. The claw of a 'C' snapped around the upright of an 'L'. There was a grotesque, almost Gothic, ugliness about the setting which must have offended the craftsman who had been commissioned to make it.

But Lester Ruddy had more urgent matters on his mind than the study of the finer points of jewellery design.

'We can cheat on the clasp, just so long as the chain looks right.' He didn't think it odd that they'd spent an entire morning on one single prop. He'd once worked as second assistant to an Italian director who had held up shooting for a week while his minions had scoured the antique shops of Venice searching for a particular silver-topped hairbrush. It had been featured in a scene that had ended up on the cutting-room floor before the film was released. Television might be crazy, but the movie industry was crazier.

'Funny,' mused Ackerman when the drama had died down, 'I wouldn't have thought Charlie was the kind of woman to get upset about a little thing like that.'

'But who knows what kind of woman Charlie is?' Liz Briley said surprisingly. 'Look at her now.'

Charlotte was mingling with the cast, laughing at one of Baxter Hadley's bad jokes while half-listening to Jane Connor's rambling discourse on the trouble she was having finding a good plumber these days.

She gave the impression of being equally interested in both Baxter's joke and Jane's plumbing problems, dispensing the bounty of her ageless charm with the effulgence of a celebrity priest blessing the faithful.

Joanna Saint-Clair hovered, as usual, efficiently on the fringes of the group, ready to be of service.

'You could have told her in advance.' There was something faintly alarming, thought John Arthur, about her steely expression.

'How were we supposed to know she'd take it so hard?'

She looked at him guardedly as if weighing up whether the remark was worthy of a reply and deciding against it.

Charlotte's rippling voice rose above the rumble of relieved chatter, the voice that could direct a whisper with perfect pitch and clarity to the gallery. 'Well, Lester, isn't it about time we got the show on the road?'

She betrayed no sign of the traumatic few hours she'd inflicted on the company. The substitute chain hung limply round her neck, curiously alien, unbelonging. She'd handed over the real thing for safe keeping to her niece Joanna, who fingered the ugly clasp with a nervous intensity out of character with her coolly negative presence.

★     ★     ★

Several weeks later on the night of April 1st, at a conservative estimate, twenty-five million people settled down in front of the television to bear avid witness to the fatal come-uppance of Chelsea Fortune in *Wild Fortune*.

Sipping a soothing brandy, Charlotte Saint-Clair watched the episode in her pretty Sussex cottage, the retreat to which she'd hardly ever retreated until her retirement from the series.

She was well pleased, but conscious of a feeling of restlessness. For a couple of weeks she'd enjoyed the peace, the walks in the woods, the pottering round the village, the long nights in which the quiet was punctuated only by the hooting of owls or the muffled sound of an occasional passing car on the lane two hundred yards away.

Then the lack of a purpose palled, the

leisureliness of a life with no sense of direction became tedious. Perhaps, after all, she thought, retirement isn't for me. Tomorrow, she decided, she'd ring up her agent and discuss some of those offers she'd told him she didn't want to hear about.

## CHAPTER FIVE

Ralph Brand, former Detective-Inspector of the Sussex Constabulary, now retired, was having much the same thoughts about his enforced idleness as he switched on the television on the night of April 1st.

At first he'd settled back with relief into the pace of an existence from which all the urgency of a paid, demanding job had been removed. A widower with no responsibilities except to himself, he could now indulge his fancy, take up all the hobbies he'd never had the time to enjoy when he was working, lie in late in the morning and sit up for the midnight movie on TV because there'd be no pressures on him to be alert at the crack of dawn. He could see the friends he'd neglected over the years, take trips abroad, sell the pokey flat on the seafront that had suited him nicely when he'd just needed to use it for bed and breakfast. Perhaps buy a neat bungalow with a bit of garden.

'I'll go fishing,' he'd told his ex-sergeant, John Waller, who, being thirty years younger, had pulled a face and warned him that he'd get fed up with that in no time flat. 'Not me, chummy,' he'd laughed. But Waller had been right. The hobbies that had seemed so inviting became boring. As the weeks went by, the thought of trips abroad for no reason beyond sightseeing lost their appeal. After a few visits to estate agents and inspections of dull little boxes on estates clustered round the coastal towns he'd decided it would be too much trouble to move anyway. A couple of persistent agents still sent him details of desirable properties which turned out to be anything but desirable, until even they couldn't be bothered to proposition such an exacting and obviously uninterested potential buyer.

He'd been glad when John Waller had been promoted to Inspector and had celebrated with the lads at the station who now all seemed absurdly young for policemen. And he envied them their enthusiasm for the job, their certain knowledge that tomorrow would be full of activity, aggro and the satisfaction of putting into practice their skills and training.

Well, he still had his pipe and his pint, he comforted himself, as he watched the final episode of *Wild Fortune*. That, too, was a sign of the time-filling waste of his retirement. He'd become addicted to TV 'soap'. But even if he hadn't, he'd have watched this particular series for Dame Charlotte Saint-Clair. Having been brought up with the cinema habit in his youth, he'd remained an incurable movie fan all his life. It had been a big joke around the station. And he well remembered the time he fell deeply and enduringly in love with Charlotte Saint-Clair. He'd been a young constable in the Metropolitan Police before the war when he'd seen her in her first starring M-G-M role opposite a major actor in something called *The Passionate Woman*. It had been a silly romance which cruelly wasted the talents of the actor, who obviously had felt it *infra dig* to play stooge in a showcase for M-G-M's British import.

As a rival to Garbo, she'd been billed thereafter as 'the passionate woman'—a trivial label which conveyed nothing of the unique, luminous quality of her arresting beauty and quicksilver emotional range. In those mesmerizing close-ups she'd seemed to communicate her yearnings and expectations to every member of the audience. When she'd died lingeringly at the end of the film, he'd felt an inconsolable sense of loss, almost as great as the loss he'd felt when his own young wife had been killed during the war. Of course, it was just a movie. It wasn't life. But in a sense she'd become part of his life from that moment. Not wanting to be thought a fool by his colleagues, he'd secretly read all the gossip items about her, followed her career in Hollywood, sat through all her films two or three times.

When she'd returned to Britain in the late 1950s he'd seen her in the theatre, a ferocious Lady Macbeth, a stunning Portia (although by then she was ideally too old for the role), a vivid Hedda Gabler, an authoritative Lady Bracknell, a raging Electra. Her versatility was constantly surprising and the beauty of youth had matured with the years, the lines of age illuminating rather than diminishing that splendid bone structure.

Once he'd nerved himself to send her a fan letter after a particularly fine performance in a Robert Bolt play. He'd been rewarded with a gracious note and a signed photograph which he'd kept hidden in the bottom drawer of his bureau. It would have been bad for his image as the 'thunderer' who struck terror into the hearts of young constables to be exposed as a devoted and constant admirer of a face on the screen, a figure on the stage.

Of course, she'd been far too good for the trashy nonsense of *Wild Fortune*, but at least it had brought her into his living-room to fuel his fantasies about her. He'd never wanted to meet her, even to see her in the flesh outside the theatre. He was content to worship from afar.

As unseen hands tightened the chain round her neck on television the camera zoomed in for a last close-up, the face contorted with terror.

The credits came up over the face, the maddeningly familiar theme music swelled and a voice reminded the audience that a new season of *Wild Fortune* would be transmitted in the autumn. But a *Wild Fortune* without Chelsea! He wondered whether Charlotte would enjoy her retirement any more than he was enjoying his.

The next morning he rose early—lying in late was a pleasure which had quickly lost its charm—and made his sparse breakfast of coffee and toast. Old habits didn't just die hard, they didn't die at all. He switched on breakfast TV. He found he relied more and more on radio and television to provide the company that was lacking from his solitary life.

From the kitchen he caught sight of the face of Charlotte Saint-Clair on the screen. Probably an item about the demise of her character which had fascinated the nation since it had first been alerted to the probability. But the face remained on the screen for longer than usual. It cut to an interview she'd given a few weeks ago, discussing her reasons for retiring from the series. Then there were flashes of still photographs from her films.

The item seemed to be going on for an unconscionable time. They were certainly getting plenty of mileage out of Chelsea Fortune's death. Though the sound was muted from where he was standing by the cooker in the

45

kitchen, the word 'murder' came over loud and clear, repeated time and again in the commentary.

With his coffee mug in his hand—cups and saucers were too much trouble—he walked out of the kitchen and planted himself in front of the set. 'As yet the police are saying nothing except that they are treating it as a case of murder.' He switched up the sound as the face of his former sparring partner, John Waller, came up on the screen, looking suitably grave. Despite the prodding of the unseen reporter he could at this time add nothing to the original statement.

The camera returned to the studio link man. 'And so with horrific irony, Charlotte Saint-Clair met her death in her Sussex cottage at the hands of an unknown assailant at the same time as the character she indelibly created was killed on the television screen and in the same manner—by strangulation with her heavy gold chain.' The florid prose remained in Brand's mind long after the rest of the news and the weather forecast. He stared unseeing at the busy screen. Charlotte Saint-Clair was dead! Even as he experienced the first shock, his brain started to tick over as it would have done had he still been an active detective-inspector.

He picked up the phone and put in a call to the station. Waller wasn't there but he left a message for him to call Ralph Brand when he returned. Then he opened the drawer of his bureau and removed the signed photograph of Charlotte Saint-Clair from beneath a pile of clean shirts and socks. He sat for several minutes gazing down at that defiantly beautiful face with the flamboyant signature scrawled across the neck and winding into the chain that had become her trademark. His eyes misted over and he felt a damp trickle weave its way down his cheek. Then he blew his nose noisily, went back into the kitchen and heated up the coffee.

When John Waller phoned Brand two hours later, he sounded decidedly edgy. Brand recognized the tone. How often he'd been guilty of the same impatience when he'd had to cope with unwanted callers in the middle of a crisis!

'You couldn't have picked a more awkward time, Ralph.'

Since Brand had retired their relationship had subtly altered: Waller, still affable, respectful, but unmistakably the senior—or, rather, superior—partner in a friendship based on years of shared experience enforcing law and order and apprehending villains. They now addressed each other as 'Ralph' and 'John', but the use of Christian names didn't come easily, tagged on the end of a greeting like a limp, uncomfortable afterthought. Too many years of observing rank couldn't be wiped out overnight.

'I can imagine you're up to your eyes,' said Brand sympathetically, deciding an apology would have stuck in his throat.

'Press, TV wallahs!' Waller sighed. 'Give me nice anonymous murders any day.'

'Makes a change from stolen cars, rowdies at the Pier Pavilion and punch-ups at the pub. Anyway it'll make you a star copper with all that TV coverage.'

'Come on, Ralph, you didn't call me for a chit-chat. And if you did, I've more important—'

'—things to do. Point taken. Let's put it this way, I'm interested.'

'Who isn't?' His voice relaxed, shedding the official tone. 'Well, you would be, wouldn't you? Movie buff like you.'

'I thought, maybe . . . you could use a bit of help.' Brand cursed himself for the clumsy way it had come out. He sounded like all the nuts who wished their services on the police when a murder was committed, enjoying an ego trip. And very rarely were they anything but a damned, time-wasting nuisance.

'Ralph,' said Waller gently, 'you're not *on* the Force any more.'

'You don't have to remind me. But an old codger with time on his hands might come in useful, poking around a bit.' That had come out wrong too. It was the whining plea of a pensioner who needed to be assured that he was needed. He wasn't an old codger. He was a trained detective with his full faculties and wits about him. Damned if he'd grovel to his former sergeant.

'Put me down as an unpaid informer,' he said brusquely. 'Tell you what, I'll buy you a pint later today. Anywhere you say.'

'Ralph, I don't even know when I'll get through.'

'Then I'll wait for you. At The Crown and Sceptre tonight.'

'I can't.'

Brand cut him off abruptly. 'You've got to have some time off. Even a half-hour. I'll be there from six-thirty all evening till closing time.'

'Well, I'll try . . .'

'See you, chummy.' He put down the receiver smartly before Waller could put up another argument.

His spirits rose. The old juices of being on a case started to flow. He did his chores and went for his constitutional, cooked his lunch and read the papers with a brisk sense of purpose he hadn't enjoyed since he'd retired. He'd made a decision. If anyone was going to solve the murder of Charlotte Saint-Clair it was going to be him, whether Waller liked it or not. He owed that much to her after all the years of second-hand pleasure she'd given to him.

In the hours before he took himself off to The Crown and Sceptre he marshalled his thoughts, itemized his questions and dug deeply into his memory for all the stray bits of information and gossip he'd stored up about Charlotte over more than four decades.

# CHAPTER SIX

Ralph Brand had been nursing his pint of best local bitter, more nourishing than the gassy stuff, for three hours when John Waller finally put in an appearance in the saloon bar of The Crown and Sceptre.

He looked drawn and harassed as he sank gratefully into the chair beside Brand.

'Usual?'

Waller nodded. He didn't utter until Brand set the foaming tankard down on the dog-eared cardboard pub coaster in front of him. He took a deep swig. 'That's better.'

Then he looked intently at Brand. Authority had etched new lines on the face which had always seemed so fresh and youthful when he was Brand's sergeant.

'I really am pressed for time, Ralph. So what's all this nonsense about lending a hand? Look at it my way, would you have liked your old superior poking his nose in on a case just because he has too much time to spare?'

Brand had prepared himself for Waller's reaction and had mentally steeled himself not to lose his temper. He was in no position to act his old role of the 'thunderer'. Sweet reason would be more likely to get the results he wanted.

'I wouldn't like it and you know it. But this isn't just a case, it's bound to be a national scandal until you nail the blighter who did it.'

Waller took a pack of cigarettes out of his pocket and lit one, taking his time deliberately.

'You're a bit late, Ralph. We *have* nailed him. At least, we think we have. Didn't you hear the evening news? Man helping the police with their inquiries?'

It was the last thing Brand expected to hear. He stared, frankly amazed, at Waller.

'Who . . . ?'

'Some poor little bugger who'd had a thing about Charlotte Saint-Clair for years. Besotted about her. Just a fan!' he said derisively.

Brand winced. Wasn't he, after all, just a fan?

'If he was such a fan why did he kill her?' He corrected himself. 'Why do you think he killed her?'

'He was seen hovering about the cottage last evening. The niece, Joanna Saint-Clair, got back about one in the morning. She'd been out with a friend. As she walked to the front door she spotted him by the open kitchen window. She called out. He turned and fled. When she let herself into the cottage, she phoned the police immediately. Then she went upstairs to Charlotte Saint-Clair's bedroom and saw her—

just as they said on TV, strangled by her own gold chain. We found him cringing under a tree in the lane by her cottage, crying.'

'Hardly evidence. Purely circumstantial,' said Brand, knowing it was the kind of strong coincidence of circumstances he'd certainly have acted upon.

'Come on, Ralph. There's a fine line between evidence and coincidence and this coincidence is way over the line. You know that. Or you ought to.'

'But it doesn't explain why.'

'If you hadn't put down the receiver this morning, I'd have told you. His own family said he was always speculating about Saint-Clair, weaving stories about her gold chain. They as near as damn it admitted he was off his rocker about her. It gets some fans that way. Look at the clown who murdered John Lennon. The niece said he was a pest. She recognized him. He was always hanging around the stage door or studio, kept writing crazy letters to her aunt, threatening, cajoling. Half of them she didn't show to Charlotte Saint-Clair because they were too upsetting. Open and shut case?'

'What does he say?'

'Not a lot. Babbling most of the time. Hopelessly deranged. There'll obviously have to be a psychiatrist's report.'

'But did he say anything?'

'Ralph, I'm not supposed to be telling you

this.' Waller shrugged. 'OK, you're not just a member of the public. He said he was drinking in a nearby pub. The Dragon, at the time of her murder.'

'Which was?'

'Between ten and eleven, as near as Grimey can tell before an autopsy.' Grimsdyke—popularly known around the station as 'Grimey'—was the police surgeon.

'That would be two hours, give or take, after the television show, the *Wild Fortune* episode.'

'Just about.'

Brand stared into the dregs of his bitter, uncertain of his own feelings. Was he glad that Charlotte's killer had been apprehended so quickly or sneakingly sad that he had no hand in his capture? For a few hours he'd persuaded himself that he had a useful reason for living. Now he was just a nosey old ex-copper with nothing to do but waste the time of a busy detective who was too kind to tell him to be quiet and buzz off.

'Where is he?' he said finally.

'We've got him here. In custody. For the moment, until he's charged.'

'Can I see him?'

'Ralph, you know better ...'

'But can I see him? You can bend the rules a little. They all know me. It wouldn't seem odd.'

'It would if the Chief Constable found out.'

'Well, he doesn't have to, does he? How many

times have we skirted round the regulations before? What the Chief doesn't know won't hurt him.'

'All right. Tomorrow morning, early. Before the hordes descend. Act like it's just a visit to me. A few minutes. No more, mind.'

Waller finished his beer and gathered up his raincoat.

'I don't know why I'm doing this, Ralph, I really don't. Can you tell me?'

'Just because,' said Brand, leaving the rest of the sentence suspended because they both knew he was doing it for all the years they'd worked together, quarrelled, closed ranks against their superiors. For all the cases Brand had solved by instinct rather than the cold reason of evidence.

'Nine, then.' Waller grinned. 'You're a rum bugger, you know that—sir?'

★　　　★　　　★

It was a crisp, bright April morning, the sun sparkling on the sea and warming the early joggers punishing their muscles on the beach, when Brand presented himself at the police station and asked for Waller.

The constable on duty knew him well.

'Can't leave the old place alone, sir.' His youth deferred to the age of the portly man in hardy tweeds in front of the desk.

'Gets to be a habit, son.'

54

'Seems we're going to be famous. TV, Press. They've been camped outside all night. Probably gone off for a jar and a slice. Not much going to happen until he's taken away. We had to sneak the niece in this morning by the back door.'

'Benson.' Waller's voice boomed at the young copper, warning him to keep his mouth shut. He sounds just like I did, thought Brand. Thunderer—Mark II. They hadn't noticed Waller silently leaving his office, catching them unawares. Just like I used to, Brand chuckled.

'Nice to see you, Ralph.' He turned to Brand as if he were greeting a caller on a social visit. 'Come on in. What news from the retirement front?'

'I like your window-dressing' said Brand when they were closeted in Waller's office. 'Put anyone off the scent.'

'He's too chatty by half, that one.'

'I expect he figures I'm no threat to security.'

'Then he'll have to learn you don't take anyone on trust.' Waller shrugged apologetically. 'Sorry, Ralph. Just one of those days.'

'How's the suspect?'

'As well as can be expected. Come on.'

He led the way to the cells in the basement of the police station; neat, sanitary cells with a modicum of comfort which had housed many a pugnacious drunk or tearaway vandal overnight, but rarely a suspected killer.

Waller nodded at the uniformed sergeant who acknowledged Brand grudgingly. They hadn't rubbed together too happily when Brand was on the Force, Ralph remembered.

The solitary inhabitant of the cell block was sitting hunched on a functional wooden chair, staring into a hostile distance, his slight body tensed, defensive. He was a small man in his middle fifties with sparse grey-speckled sandy hair. His melancholy watery eyes dominated a face that would be lost in a crowd. As the sergeant unlocked the cell door, a low whisper escaped from his thin lips.

He didn't look like a killer, thought Brand. But then what killer did?

'What's his name?' muttered Brand, cupping his hand over his mouth.

'William Richards.'

The man looked at Waller, then fixed those sad, fanatical eyes on Brand. And it was to Brand that he addressed his plea. 'I wouldn't harm her. I wouldn't harm a hair of her head. I don't kill a fly, even a fly. All God's creatures. We're all God's creatures.' He rocked to and fro in the chair, his arms hanging limply by his sides as if they didn't belong to him.

'Believe! Believe! You believe me.' He spoke with sudden, hard authority directly to Brand.

'William,' said Brand softly, but the man seemed not to hear. Waller gripped Brand's elbow and tapped his own forehead with his free hand. 'I told you. Mental.'

'I heard that. I heard that.' With surprising agility the prisoner leapt out of his chair and grippd Brand's wrists before Waller could stop him.

'Don't,' warned Brand. Waller paused in the act of calling the sergeant. Brand, he knew of old, had his ways.

'Tell me, where were you the night before last? You remember the night, don't you— Billy?' By some knowing instinct, Brand had hit on the name to which William Richards was accustomed. The man responded, granting him a grateful, wintry smile.

'You went to Charlotte Saint-Clair's cottage, didn't you, Billy?'

The man nodded once, then again more firmly, remembering.

'And where else, Billy?'

'Where else?' He furrowed his brow, dredging deep into his addled brain for a clue. 'The pub. I was there. They don't believe me— but I'm sure I was there. Wasn't I?' He looked to Brand for reassurance that the pub wasn't just another of his fantasies.

'Time up, Ralph. You've had your few minutes.'

Gently, Brand loosened the hands that were still gripping his wrists. 'That's all right, Billy,' he said. At the cell door he turned and looked searchingly at the lost, lonely figure standing on the concrete floor, his hands reaching out as if for a miracle.

'I knew I should never have let you see him,' said Waller irritably as they returned to his office. 'I knew you'd . . .'

'What?'

'I don't know. Give him hope.'

'Is that so bad?'

'It is when all the evidence—'

'—circumstantial,' Brand corrected him.

'—all the evidence points to the fact that he murdered Charlotte Saint-Clair. But that's not for us to decide. After today, it's up to the lawyers and judge and jury.'

'You're pretty sure the evidence is sufficient for him to be charged?'

'I've known cases of men being charged on far flimsier evidence.'

'What about the pub? Surely . . .'

'Don't tell me my job, Ralph. We found his fingerprints in Saint-Clair's bedroom. The pub proprietor and his wife can't recall him being there that evening. And even if he was, what does that prove?'

'It would prove he was speaking the truth.'

'Ralph, you don't change, do you? You treat facts as if they were a sort of enemy.'

'Not an enemy. They just cloud the issue. Facts are like the surface glaze on an old oil painting. When you chip it away you get to the real thing. Not always, I grant you. But quite often.'

'The past, always the past.'

'That's where the secrets lie. I don't suppose I can see what I assume you're now calling the murder weapon?'

'You don't ask much, do you?'

'Come on, John, just a look.'

'Just this—and no more, Ralph.'

With barely concealed exasperation Waller put in a call which led to a discussion and then grudging agreement.

The gold rope with its strange, ugly clasp was now encased in a clinical polythene bag with a tag attached to it. It no longer had any identity beyond the lethal purpose to which it had been put.

'It doesn't look much, does it?' said Brand. 'But such is the stuff that legends are made of.'

'Legends?'

'She was never without it. For thirty years. Did you know that, John?'

'I suppose I must have. But it's hardly significant. It's just the chain that did her in.'

'Then you don't know much, old chummy, you don't know much.'

He peered closely at the clasp. Amethysts— for mourning. Had 'C' and 'L'—the letters in the clasp—been joined in some shared mourning? Or did Charlotte Saint-Clair just like

59

amethysts, a humble stone for a relatively wealthy lady?

He thanked John Waller profusely—more profusely than he'd intended—as he left. He had a feeling he'd be needing Waller's goodwill again before this case was over.

Outside the police station, a posse of reporters and photographers were camped on the pavement, their nose for news alerting them that something was about to happen.

At that moment a youngish woman with a plain, efficient face which bore the weary traces of recent shock was being escorted to the door by the Superintendent. Brand recognized her as Joanna Saint-Clair, Charlotte's niece. A constable hustled her through the mob to the tune of clicking cameras and barked questions. She waved them away with practised competence, the result of many years of dealing with the Press dogging her aunt.

As she passed, her glance met Brand's. There was a puzzled, uncertain expression on her face as if she were posing her own questions and not finding answers.

Whatever was bothering her overlaid the grief she must have felt over her aunt's obscenely topical death. Watching her intently as she elbowed her way through the army of media reporters, Brand had the nagging suspicion there was much more to the case of Charlotte Saint-Clair's murder than the besotted, half-crazed man he'd just left in that bleak basement cell.

## CHAPTER SEVEN

In the rearview mirror of the nippy tan Mini which she'd obstinately refused to exchange for a more up-to-date model, Joanna Saint-Clair caught sight of her face, a grim smile relaxing the stern, angular features. She congratulated herself on putting the Press off the scent. That nice Inspector Waller had been helpful. 'Give her a chance, boys. She's nothing more to tell you beyond what you already know,' he'd said. And maybe they'd believed him. Well, he was right in one respect, she thought. She'd nothing more to tell *them*. Not yet, anyway.

Besides, if they'd followed her, they might have risked missing the sight of that pathetic creature being transferred from the police station to the temporary security of prison, after he was charged. She imagined him, bewildered, trying to cover his face. Or maybe he didn't even know enough to attempt to disguise his identity. She felt an inexplicable pity for him, inexplicable because there seemed no question that he had murdered her aunt. If any evidence had weighted the scales against him it had been hers.

She was too absorbed in her thoughts to

61

notice in the wing mirror an unremarkable maroon Subaru sedan keeping a measured distance behind her. As she drove, fast but with due care, through the spring green Sussex countryside, skirting Findon Valley and the Iron Age Cissbury Ring, the Subaru allowed a lorry and a few impatient cars to overtake it. Ralph Brand was a skilled hand at tailing a quarry without arousing suspicion. The sparkling tan of the Mini ahead of him advertised itself at every turn of the road.

He noticed with relief that she passed the all but hidden detour which would have led to Charlotte Saint-Clair's retreat. He'd doubted that she'd go back to the home she'd shared with her aunt, but if she had he'd have been confronted by legions of reporters and police crawling all over the place and he hadn't yet sorted out a plausible reason for turning up at the scene of the crime.

The mini zigzagged through the lanes, cosseted in hedgerows and trees sprouting the first leafy promise of summer, until, a few miles on, it came to rest outside a neat flint cottage nestling in one of those secluded Sussex villages that surprise the traveller who strays off the bypass.

Brand parked some yards away, certain he hadn't been observed, filled and lit the pipe that always seemed to put his mind in order. Instinct had made him follow Joanna Saint-Clair.

Instinct and that puzzled look he'd glimpsed on her face outside the police station. Whether Billy Richards had been capable of killing the star he'd apparently worshipped for years, Brand couldn't be sure. He'd investigated too many murders, interrogated too many suspects who'd fooled him into believing them innocent until the evidence proved them irrevocably guilty, to make snap judgements. But from his brief few minutes with Richards he'd been conscious of a niggling doubt. It was all too pat, too easy. The man had practically begged to be arrested. Well, that wasn't unusual either. Crimes of passion like this one carried heavy burdens of guilt that had to be exorcized.

And perhaps he'd have taken the evidence at face value, as Waller had, if he hadn't happened to see Joanna Saint-Clair at that exact moment before she'd had time to compose herself for the waiting Press.

He watched her get out of the Mini, lock the door prudently and let herself into the cottage. There was nothing very special about it. It had been nicely restored, but it had the unadopted look of a place that housed transitory visitors. Perhaps a rented home whose owners let it out for winter residence and holidays.

After a decent interval of twenty minutes, Brand tapped out the dead tobacco from his pipe in the ashtray, got out of the car and trod the uneven pavement to the front door. The cottage didn't have a bell, so he thumped the wood panelling firmly. After a moment or two, the door was opened by a tall, tousled man in his early forties, wearing a baggy sweater and jeans. His lean, wary face and brown, grey-flecked hair looked vaguely familiar.

'What do you want?' He spoke in the trained voice of an actor or a lawyer or, indeed, a clergyman: a man used to communicating with an audience. There was an underlying aggressiveness in his curt inquiry. Brand made a mental note to keep his own temper in check. He didn't want to risk having the door slammed in his face.

'Who is it, Russ?' a woman's voice called from the interior of the cottage, followed by its owner who, catching sight of Brand, groaned: 'Oh God, not another of those . . .'

'No, Miss Saint-Clair, I'm not from the Press.'

'Then who the hell are you?' her companion, Russ whoever-he-was, said with what seemed to Brand an undue show of hostility. After all, he might as well have been canvassing for the Labour Party or calling to read the gas meter.

The man cupped his hand round the door frame, effectively barring the entrance and protecting the woman at his elbow.

In the few minutes she'd been inside the cottage she'd unpinned her hair which hung loosely to her shoulders, softening the austere jawline. She looked younger, more vulnerable than the capable young woman who had dealt so firmly with the reporters outside the police station.

'I'm from the police,' said Brand, which wasn't exactly the truth but close enough, he hoped, to get himself a hearing. He could declare his interest later. He held his breath waiting to see whether they'd exercise their rights by insisting he show his credentials.

But the word 'police' seemed enough for the moment. It invariably was in his experience. He quickly improved his advantage. 'From Inspector Waller,' he continued, and that was reasonably accurate too. A small white lie would be easier to explain away than a whopper when the reckoning came.

'I've just come from the station.'

'I know, Miss Saint-Clair. So have I. My name's Brand. We—I—felt it would be more comfortable to talk here. Away from all the reporters. It couldn't have been very pleasant for you.'

'The Superintendent didn't say anything about...'

'Please, Miss Saint-Clair. Just a few minutes of your time, I promise.' He inched himself closer to the grudgingly half-opened door. 'Could I perhaps come inside?'

Joanna Saint-Clair and the man named Russ exchanged anxious glances, then she shrugged.

'Well, if you must. But I've told your people everything I know.'

'Jo, you don't have to,' the man argued, his arm still guarding the entrance.

She turned on him sharply. 'Don't *you* start in, Russ. Let's get it over with.'

The front door led straight into a square, sparsely furnished living-room. A faded rug decorated the stone-flagged floor, a three-piece suite which had seen better days was grouped unimaginatively in front of a pokey fireplace that housed a gas fire. A chipped oval table had been shunted into a corner with four hard, upright chairs placed with military precision around it.

Joanna Saint-Clair caught Brand's practised eye taking in the details of the room. 'Russ has been renting it for a while,' she explained casually, excusing the meagreness of the accommodation.

'Nice and close to Charlotte—your aunt's home.'

She looked up at him abruptly. 'What does that mean?'

'Nothing, nothing at all. I just assume he's a friend of yours and wanted to be near you, as you were staying with your aunt.'

'That's a bloody lie!' The man's aggression threatened to explode into something nastier.

'Oh, come on, Russ, give over.' She seemed adept at soothing this prickly display of temper.

'It's not a lie. What's the point of secrecy? Sooner or later, someone would have found us out.' She regretted the admission and the manner in which it was expressed instantly. 'I don't seem to know *what* I'm saying, Mr ... Brand, did you say?'

'Inspector.' Another white lie to explain away, he cursed.

'It's just all been so sudden,' she went on, 'so shocking. During the past twenty-four hours I feel as if I've been taking part in some awful thriller and you find yourself speaking like a character in a thriller. Found us out!' she repeated. 'All I meant was that Russ and I have been friends for a long time.'

'And your aunt didn't approve?'

'I didn't say that. But, well, it happens. It happens in the best regulated circles.' She smiled cynically.

'And it seemed a good idea to have a secret rendezvous?'

She smiled again with more humour at his Victorian turn of phrase. 'You could call it that. There's nothing very sinister about it.'

'Of course not.' Brand could sense the growing anger of the man restlessly pacing the distance between the fireplace and the front door. He tried to remember where and when he'd felt that aura of personal tension on a more public occasion. Then it clicked. Russ! Russ Gilchrist. He'd seen him often on television in the kind of featured roles that make an impression but not the name of the actor. There were dozens of serviceable actors like Gilchrist: recognizable faces in the crowd whose names elude you.

Brand set aside for the moment the interesting speculation whether Russ's tension was the result of long years of professional frustration or whether it was due to a more immediate concern. He mustered instead a charming show of surprise. 'It's Russ Gilchrist, isn't it? Thought I knew you. Admire your work very much. That last thing you did ... what was it?'

'*Nightmares in the Dark,*' Russ volunteered, almost amiably.

'That's it. *Nightmares in the Dark*. The scene where you can't...' Brand was groping into a barely remembered impression of a routine made-for-TV movie he'd seen not long ago. But he was pretty sure Gilchrist would fill in the gaps.

His small experience of actors had taught Brand that they were usually blessed with instant recall of all their roles.

Gilchrist's eyes lit up. '... where I can't understand why she acted so strangely when her husband left home?'

'Exactly. Unusual reaction. I liked the way you shifted gears—emotionally, I mean.'

Gilchrist raised his hands in a gesture of

triumph. 'There, you see'. He turned to Joanna Saint-Clair. 'This is a member of the public. I told that sodding director it was the only way to play it.'

She nodded, sweetly, with the sort of affection a mother lavishes on a truant child who, against the odds, has done well in his exams.

If Brand had wondered what she saw in Gilchrist that glance, in part, explained it. He doubted whether Charlotte Saint-Clair had ever needed or wanted that kind of reassurance. Years of living with her aunt's self-sufficiency must have created a yearning in Joanna Saint-Clair to be of use to someone in more than the purely material way in which she serviced the legend of a great star.

'Of course you were right, Russ,' she said softly. She glanced at Brand and he sensed in her look a silent thank-you for comforting the ego of her chronically insecure friend. Gilchrist touched her cheek gently. 'Good old Jo,' he murmured.

As their eyes locked, Brand felt uncomfortably *de trop*. On another occasion, he'd have made a graceful exit. But this wasn't the moment to retreat. And, even while he admired her handling of Gilchrist, he found Joanna Saint-Clair's easy submersion of grief at her aunt's death both intriguing and unnerving.

He noisily settled himself in one of the ugly

armchairs by the fireplace. A dislocating spring lodged itself rather painfully in the fleshy back of his spine but he endured the discomfort stoically.

'It must be a fascinating life,' he said fatuously, bringing them back to his unwelcome presence, although he felt he might have broken the ice of their suspicion.

'It is—when you're working,' Gilchrist said sullenly.

They seemed mildly surprised that he had insinuated himself into the room so firmly: an unbudgeable fixture by the fireplace.

The gentle softness drained out of Joanna Saint-Clair's expression.

'Just what did you want to see me about, Inspector?' Then another and more alarming thought apparently struck her. 'And how did you know I was here? I didn't give this address to the police. I said I'd be at the London flat if they wanted me. I didn't want to go back to that other place—the cottage.'

'That was rather remiss of you, if I may say so.'

'It was none of their business. But you haven't answered my question.'

Brand took a deep breath. It was time for the truth. He hoped it would be a truth she'd accept in the spirit in which it was offered.

'I followed you.'

'Then . . . you . . .'

'He's not from the police. Where's his identification?' Again, there was the warning of uncontrollable anger in Gilchrist's voice.

Calmly, Brand ignored it and turned his full attention to Joanna Saint-Clair who was regarding him quizzically, waiting.

'I am from the police. But not quite *of* the police. Any more, that is. Inspector Waller used to be my sergeant before I retired from the Force.'

'How can I believe that?'

Brand foraged in his wallet and drew out a blue card. Still keeping his eyes on Joanna Saint-Clair, he handed it to Gilchrist.

'National Association of Retired Police Officers. Brand,' Gilchrist read. 'A goddamned geriatric prying copper. Get out. You've no authority to barge in here. Get that Waller chap on the phone, Jo.'

He flung the unassuming square of cardboard into Brand's lap.

Brand continued to stare steadily at the woman.

The corners of her mouth twitched, whether with rage or amusement Brand couldn't yet tell. But at least she wasn't sharing Gilchrist's hotheaded response to Brand's duplicity. Perhaps his earlier elaborate interest in Gilchrist's acting ability had paid off, winning him her trust.

'There isn't a phone, Russ,' she reminded him coolly. 'There's a box in the village or

71

at the pub.'

'Just leave, then!'

'Do you want me to leave, Miss Saint-Clair?'

She considered for a moment, then finally she said: 'I'm curious, *Mr* Brand.' She stressed the Mr Provokingly. 'Why would a retired Inspector waste his time following me and gaining entry—I believe that's the term—to talk to me about a case that doesn't concern him? I don't imagine your Inspector Waller would be very pleased either, am I right, Mr Brand?'

Brand smiled, took out his pipe and tobacco pouch. 'Do you mind?' She shook her head. 'You're not wrong. Inspector Waller would be furious. But he'll get over it, because we've worked together for years and he trusts my instinct even when I'm not being paid to employ it.'

'And what does your instinct tell you, Mr Brand?'

'That you're no more happy about that man in the cell than I am. I saw the look on your face as you came out of the police station.'

'Of course she's not happy about him—he murdered her aunt.' In his blundering way Gilchrist had provided the answer that could have sent Brand packing forever. And Joanna Saint-Clair knew it.

'Doesn't that seem logical to you, Mr Brand?' she said, but she spoke as if they were discussing an academic question, not a good reason for showing him the door.

'Eminently logical. But the case isn't proved until he's been tried and found guilty. Do you mind if I put my cards on the table, Miss saint-Clair?'

'I think it's about time,' she replied.

Puffing on his pipe, Brand sank back into the armchair, wincing slightly at the damage the wayward spring was doing to his ample behind.

Despite some exasperated interruptions from Russ Gilchrist, she listened attentively to Brand's explanation of his interest in Charlotte Saint-Clair's murder. He left nothing out, speaking as unemotionally as he could.

When he'd finished, Joanna Saint-Clair was silent, staring out of the cottage window that fronted the cobbled village pavement.

She picked up a trivial china ornament of a clown that had been left behind probably by some previous tenant. 'A fan!' she said with a trace of humour. 'Just like that poor devil in the cell.'

If he were still capable of blushing, Brand would have blushed. He'd gambled on her understanding but even as he was talking he knew he risked her ridicule.

'What do you want from me, Mr Brand?'

'Help.'

'How can I help you? And why should I? Surely the police are perfectly capable of handling the case?'

'Perfectly capable,' he agreed.

'What can you contribute that they can't?'

'Maybe—time. Patience.'

'And love?' she asked shrewdly.

Brand shrugged, his defences down. 'That too. I want you to help me know Charlotte Saint-Clair.'

'Everyone knew Charlotte Saint-Clair.'

'I don't think they did. I'm not a *voyeur*, a silly old man raking over the ashes for his own satisfaction.'

She studied him so carefully that he began to be embarrassingly aware of the trickle of ash flecking down his lapel. 'I don't believe you are. But are you on my side?'

The startling remark caught Brand momentarily off-balance. Was he on her side, as she put it? And what was her 'side'? It was a fresh, disturbing development he hadn't anticipated. He looked into those arresting eyes of hers and, finding no answer there, improvised his own, relying on instinct.

'Yes, Miss Saint-Clair, I think I am.'


## CHAPTER EIGHT

For the first time since Brand had forced his way into Russ Gilchrist's pokey little hideaway in this unprepossessing village off the busy A24,

Joanna Saint-Clair smiled broadly. He noticed with surprise that she had a dimple in her left cheek which gave her face a girlish, unfinished look, as if it were waiting for maturity to flesh it out. Not for the first time he marvelled what a cool customer she was. If she felt any grief over her aunt's death she was keeping it carefully hidden. Or maybe she was one of those women who had learned over years of punishing experience to keep her emotions hidden.

'You must have been a very trusting policeman, Mr Brand,' she said lightly. He couldn't be sure whether she was taunting or testing him. Either way her unexpected comment required an explanation.

'I was just wondering, Miss Saint-Clair, what you meant by your "side" of the case.'

'But that didn't stop you saying you support it. No, sorry, you *think* you do. Must be accurate. Anything I say may be taken down in evidence and used against me.' She *was* taunting him, playing him like a fish on a hook. Well, he wouldn't give her the satisfaction of squirming. He amazed himself by finding her rather admirable. Not many people would have reacted to his unwarranted intrusion with such aplomb. He knew she was intrigued and sensed that she was probably sympathetic to him, even if perhaps against her better judgement.

Deliberately he stayed silent. Two could play at this game and he was probably more experienced at it than she.

The smile and the dimple faded and the girlishness fled from the face.

'You're right, I'm being stupidly mysterious, aren't I? Just now and then I like to conjure up little mysteries for myself instead of coping with other people's mysteries.' Which created another mystery, but Brand decided to leave that one in abeyance.

She flicked a restless hand through her long hair. 'It's really very simple. If that little man the police have arrested didn't murder Charlotte, I imagine I'd be their first suspect. It's rather convenient that he was so available, as if he were begging to be arrested.'

'If he is guilty that wouldn't be unnatural. Most murderers aren't cold-blooded killers. Usually they regret their crime as soon as it's committed, not because of the victim, but because of their own sense of guilt. It's a hideous burden, you know.' Why did she have this effect on him, compelling him to reassure her?

'I didn't know. I've never murdered anyone, Inspector.' There was a subtle change in her tone as she addressed him by his old rank for the first time, as if she were beginning to accept an authority he didn't rightly deserve. He slipped easily into the role she'd conferred on him; the role he'd resigned when he'd handed in his warrant card.

'Then why would you be a suspect?'

'*Cherchez la femme!* And *la femme* might appear to be me. It won't be a secret much longer that I inherit all her worldly goods—except for a few minor bequests. The London flat, the cottage, her jewels and a great deal of money very wisely invested. She told me so and I've no reason to doubt her. She put it rather nicely, I thought: "You've put up with me for so long you deserve some reward." Then she rounded it off with a typical Charlotte let-down: "Besides I've no one else to leave it to." Don't give me one of your looks, Inspector. Oh yes, I've noticed them. Keen, searching, but not giving anything away.'

Brand allowed himself a quiet smirk. She was not only cool, but sharp, too.

'Charlotte Saint-Clair was a much loved lady. But she'd have to be a saint not to be a trial now and then, particularly to the person who had to put up with her occasional private tantrums, listen to her complaints about this one or that one which she wouldn't voice in public. And she wasn't above reminding me on very fraught occasions that I didn't have a penny to my name and wouldn't be living in relative luxury if she hadn't adopted me when my parents died. The adoption bit, by the way, was one of her fantasies. She didn't adopt me, she just inherited me and put me to good use.'

'Why are you telling me all this, Miss Saint-

Clair? There's no need.'

'If I didn't, someone would. And I don't imagine I'm your only port of call. Although God knows why you should be bothering.'

Gilchrist, who had been sitting sullenly on the edge of one of the uncomfortable chairs listening to Joanna's confessions about her relationship with her aunt, suddenly exploded. The tendons in his neck stood out like taut ropes of steel barely contained by the fragile skin.

'Stop it, Jo! You bloody fool. You don't have to talk to him. You can tell him to go to hell. And if you won't, I will.' There was a note of ferocity in his voice which should have warned Brand that, even momentarily, the man was beyond reason.

'Russ, don't!'

He rushed out of the room into what Brand assumed must be the bedroom. For a moment Brand thought he was merely sulking, but Joanna's obvious alarm suggested something more than concern over a tiresome show of temper.

When Gilchrist returned to the living-room he was brandishing a pistol, boldly, aggressively, like a character in some TV cop series in which life was cheap and didn't have to be accounted for. The sight of the weapon in the hands of the unstable Gilchrist sent a shiver of well-remembered fear through Brand. The silence in that shabby room was deafening in its menace.

Brand used the silence to observe Gilchrist. There was no knowing whether he was capable of using the pistol, but, as he waved it around ineptly, Brand judged with a silent prayer that there was no real intent to cause harm. But he was taking no chances.

'Calm down, laddie,' he said softly, his tone conciliatory from long practice. 'Don't want to upset the lady, do we? We're just having a little conversation. Nothing for the record.'

As dramatically as it had erupted, the fight seemed to go out of Gilchrist. He looked at Joanna, pleading, as if for forgiveness.

'He's right, Russ. Don't be silly. Put that thing away. I've told you...' She pulled herself up abruptly as if aware that she was saying too much. 'Put it away,' she repeated.

The pistol hung limply from Gilchrist's nervous fingers, his sudden, brief fury spent, leaving him drained and pliant. His husky body seemed to have shrunk into its bones; the lines of age, carefully concealed before, deepened, giving his face a look of wizened hopelessness.

'It's just hearing you go on about that bitch. They're all bitches in this business. Ackerman. Charlotte. All of them,' he whined.

She took him in her arms, cradling his head on her shoulder. 'I don't deserve you, Jo,' he sobbed.

The spectacle of the man, no longer young,

79

exposing his emotions so cruelly, embarrassed Brand. He'd seen it all before but it never ceased to affect him. He wished he hadn't provoked it. But Joanna Saint-Clair appeared to be used to it.

'Never mind, Russ. It's over now,' she said soothingly. 'Why don't you nip down to the pub? They're still open.'

Gilchrist straightened himself up, consciously ridding himself of all traces of his extraordinary outburst. Unless, thought Brand, he was a better actor than he'd given him credit for.

'What about him?' said Gilchrist. Brand averted his eyes from what he'd good reason to suppose was an ugly, accusing look.

'I'll manage,' she assured him. Grudgingly, Gilchrist made for the front door and banged it ear-shatteringly behind him.

'Nervy chap,' said Brand.

She picked up the pistol which had slipped out of his hand to the floor and shrugged.

'Actors enjoy playing good scenes. I should know. I've been at the receiving end of a lot of them.'

She studied Brand with that tantalizing, amused expression of hers, but again there was an underlying gratitude for his calm handling of the anxious situation.

'I gather you don't know many actors, Mr Brand.' No longer referred to as 'Inspector' he felt as if he were being charmingly but sharply put back in his place.

80

'Only by repute.'

'Well, they do sometimes carry their roles around with them. It relieves the tedium of waiting for the phone to ring. Particularly poor Russ. It doesn't ring very often for him these days.'

'I hope he's got a licence for that pistol. Even when people don't mean to fire them, they're dangerous things to have around.'

'He says he has.'

'Well, I'd make sure, if I were you. It's a criminal offence, you know, if he hasn't.'

'I'll make sure.' She assumed her competent, private secretary demeanour which, he imagined, had intimidated many a would-be intruder on Charlotte Saint-Clair's valuable time. 'Was there anything else you wanted to talk about?'

'Not really. But as I said, your help might be useful. I'd like to talk to the producer of the TV series. Sam Ackerman, isn't it?'

'You know very well it is. Because Russ mentioned him, I suppose? Russ rages about everyone who's ever turned him down for a job. Ackerman did. Ages ago.'

'I'd still like to talk to him. But not about Russ. About Charlotte Saint-Clair. He must have known her pretty well.'

'That he did. But why can't you just bamboozle your way in as you did today?'

'Because it would be so much easier if you

introduced me—over the phone, that is.'

'You want me to give you a reference.' He knew she was enjoying mocking him, but in a kindly manner. 'One retired police inspector with an insatiable curiosity about the killing of Charlotte Saint-Clair, doubts whether the prime suspect is guilty, eminently trustworthy. Something like that do?'

'It wouldn't hurt.'

She looked him up and down again in that disconcerting manner.

'All right. I'll tell him to expect you. God knows why. Maybe I do trust you. Maybe it's rather touching. An esteemed—at least I assume you're esteemed—former inspector who is a fan of the great star until death—and beyond.'

'You make it sound very silly.'

'I intended it to. It is.'

As she saw him to the door, Brand felt himself dismissed like a small boy who'd been granted the courtesy of an autograph. He was learning that the first requisite of detective work without official sanction was an ability to swallow your pride.

★     ★     ★

The meeting in Sam Ackerman's office was languishing into repetition. There was really no reason for it but Mack Tully had insisted. John Arthur, Liz Briley, Elaine Pelham were listening with marked lack of interest to his droning recital of complaints and arguments. Ackerman had suggested that Elaine attend because if the Regent TV powers-that-be agreed there should be further series of *Wild Fortune* she would certainly inherit the role of star. It was hardly likely that they wouldn't. Any publicity was good publicity and, in the callous reckoning of show business, the kind of publicity generated by Charlotte Saint-Clair's murder was a positive bonanza.

'Surely a Press conference is a bit extreme, Mack,' Liz groaned for the umpteenth time. 'There's the funeral and the memorial service, not to mention the trial to get through. Isn't that enough?'

'It's all right for you,' Mack grumbled. 'But I've had everybody on to me—the Press, TV news, radio. The Hearst newspaper group are even flying in Gloria Beesley to cover the case. She knew Charlotte well.'

'Christ! I thought she was dead,' sighed Ackerman.

'Well, she isn't. The damned old queen of the gossip columns is still very much alive, creaking a bit, but alive.'

'But what would be the point of a Press conference?' Even Elaine's agreeable calm was beginning to wear a little thin around the edges.

'Press reception,' Mack corrected her. 'Conference sounds—well, formal. Reception sounds . . .'

'Informal?' John Arthur volunteered mockingly.

Mack flashed an angry grimace in his direction. 'Stop taking the mickey.'

'Sorry.' Arthur went back to his eternal doodling.

'This way we can mop up the whole operation in one go.'

Ackerman winced. 'You really do have a charming turn of phrase.'

'What I meant was that we could all be on hand to answer questions about Charlotte, how she'd affected our lives, what a tragedy her death is. Oh, for God's sake, you know the kind of thing the Press likes. Human interest. And, of course, plans for the future from Sam.'

'There aren't any yet.'

'Well, make some up. Speculation.'

'We can't discuss the murder. *Sub judice.*'

'We don't have to discuss the murder. I know that. But you must realize I'm thinking of all of you. One big Press reception will stop you being bothered by reporters for exclusive interviews.'

'Well, I suppose there's some sense in it,' Ackerman conceded. 'I'll take it up with the gentlemen upstairs. Just one thing. Don't underestimate some nosey reporter who's done his homework asking any questions that some of you might find awkward.'

'What's that supposed to mean?' said Liz

84

sharply.

'Put it this way: Charlotte had a long life and a long career and you don't manage either without stepping on a few toes along the way. We're all agreed she was a great lady, a consummate actress, a beloved colleague. Let's make sure nothing comes out to—how can I put it?—sully that reputation. If you've anything you'd rather keep quiet about, do just that. Keep it quiet.'

For a long moment the five of them were silent, until Elaine spoke.

'You sound as if you're accusing us of harbouring a grievance against Charlotte.'

'I'm not accusing anyone of anything. I'm just warning you that the Press aren't daft, even if they seem to be sometimes.'

'Poor Liz,' chuckled John Arthur. 'What a pity you swore you'd kill that woman so publicly and so often.'

'And what a pity it was you who devised the method by which she, or Chelsea Fortune, should be killed,' Liz rounded on him bitterly.

Elaine studied her immaculately manicured fingernails. 'Now you are behaving like idiots.'

'And you haven't got so much to be cheerful about either. What was it Charlotte said about you when you joined the series? "A pushy would-be star—they're the worst kind." Engraved on my heart, like "Calais".' Liz smiled sweetly.

'That's *enough*,' barked Ackerman. 'We've all

said and done things we're not proud of. But let's just agree to be a bereaved, united company. All right, Mack, set it up and I'll get the OK. Now bugger off, the lot of you, I've got some dotty old retired police inspector coming round. Seems he's interested in Charlotte. Joanna asked me to see him as a favour.'

'Now there's a lady to reckon with, too,' said Liz.

'You are a dear thing today, love, aren't you?' John Arthur picked up his doodle pad and walked purposefully towards the door. 'You know something funny? No one has yet said how genuinely sad they are that Charlotte Saint-Clair is dead.'

## CHAPTER NINE

In the busy pub a few steps away from the Regent TV offices, Ralph Brand sipped his pint of bitter and munched without relish on a ham sandwich left over from lunch-time. It was just past evening opening time and already it was filling up with commuters, nipping in for a quick one to brace themselves for the strap-hanging journey home by tube or bus, two late shoppers with bundles of polythene bags, and stray staff from the BBC facing evening duty at Portland Place.

Brand gave up the uneven battle with the ham sandwich and left it half eaten on the plate. He attacked the bitter gratefully. It had been a wearing day and it wasn't over yet. After leaving Joanna Saint-Clair and her itchy-fingered friend, he'd driven up the A24 and parked the Subaru at Hammersmith, taking the tube the rest of the way to Oxford Circus. For a few idle minutes he allowed himself the enjoyment of breathing in the sights and sounds of the metropolis which he'd abandoned so many years before to 'bury himself', as his Super had said, in Sussex. His service in the Metropolitan Police seemed aeons ago. He looked back on it from a distance that couldn't be measured in time or geography. Was that younger man so full of ideals, bursting with enthusiasm for his job, keen, ambitious, really himself? He observed him as he might watch a character in a play, amused, objective, even sympathetically. But he could no longer identify with him.

Joanna Saint-Clair had implied that he was a silly old fool trying to regain some of the past authority by playing private detective, when he should be tending a garden, taking up harmless hobbies and behaving like retired people were supposed to behave. Perhaps she was right, he mused. Waller was satisfied with his suspect and he was an astute policeman. Brand should know. He'd trained him. So why should he, Brand, be so anxious to disbelieve what seemed to be hard evidence? He knew his motives for meddling were faintly ridiculous, even to himself.

In a sense he was pursuing shadows: a vision on a screen, a figure on a stage. If Charlotte Saint-Clair had been real to him it would have made more sense. If she'd been a relative, a dear friend, perhaps a close neighbour, his concern about her death and her killer would have been understandable. But he could claim no relationship with her beyond that of thousands, perhaps millions, of other people who didn't know her.

He chuckled quietly to himself. Joanna Saint-Clair, that clever lady, had been right again. He was a fan, just a fan, like deranged Billy Richards in that bare cell. That was the bond they had in common. Maybe that's why he couldn't bring himself to believe that Billy had murdered the object of his obsession. Reason told him it was entirely possible. Time and again he'd investigated cases of people who'd killed the object they most loved—out of passion, misunderstanding, jealousy.

But reason had never figured very heavily in Brand's calculations, when instinct told him otherwise. 'Brand's riding one of his hobbyhorses,' they used to say at the station. And the Super and the Chief Constable had let him go on riding it, albeit with some exasperation, because so often his instinct had proved him right. But now he was on his own, out on a limb. Waller would be sympathetic, bend a few rules for him, but he couldn't count on his support.

He drained the last drops of bitter. Well, he might be a silly old fool, but he was a silly old fool with more than forty years of police training behind him. Technically he might be retired, but intellectually, professionally and, yes, emotionally, he wasn't.

As he eased himself out of the throng, the early drinkers considerately made a path for him, pausing in whatever vital conversation or newly-heard joke they were spinning into the smoky atmosphere. They didn't get many pensioners in the pub and, glimpsing their own future, they paid due respect.

The glossy girl at the reception desk, her deadpan face an uncrackable mask of skilfully applied make-up, directed him to the office on the top floor after ascertaining that Sam Ackerman was waiting for him. She sized him up shrewdly as a candidate for a bit part in the series if and when it took the air again, then returned to the urgent business of filing a wayward hangnail.

As he took the lift Brand realized he'd no clear idea how the interview would develop. It didn't bother him. Every interview was different, taking its direction from the vibrations in the relationship, a sudden phrase hastily dropped, impossible to retrieve.

The voice that answered Brand's knock on Ackerman's door reassured him. Strong, guttural, marginally welcoming.

'Mr Brand. Or should I say Detective-Inspector Brand? Never sure whether policemen carry on their ranks into retirement—like Army officers.' Ackerman held out his hand to Brand. The grasp was firm and friendly. Joanna Saint-Clair must have given him a decent reference, thought Brand.

'Mr's fine. I might as well say straight away, I've no authority. I'm just grateful you agreed to see me.'

The two men regarded each other and liked what they saw. Ackerman's square, craggy face, scarred by the pressures of experience in his profession, had the lived-in quality that appealed to Brand: a portrait begging to be painted in oils by a Graham Sutherland.

And Brand's old-fashioned, comforting assurance reminded Ackerman of the coppers of his youth. No smart-assed, out-of-touch experts, but Dixons of Dock Green all. Both knew that face value was no judge of character. But if appearances were deceptive, at least they were a handy basis for communication between strangers.

'I'm afraid I haven't much time.' Ackerman indicated the one easy chair in the office.

'I appreciate that.'

Ackerman settled himself behind his desk.

'Incidentally I've just had a friend of yours on the phone.'

Brand allowed himself a puzzled frown. 'I didn't think Miss Saint-Clair . . .'

'Oh, not Joanna. A Detective-Inspector Waller. I don't think he trusts us people in the media too much. Said he hoped we wouldn't be putting out too many statements to the Press. Might hamper due process. That kind of thing.'

So, Waller had got to him first, thought Brand. Well, he supposed it was to be expected.

'He's right, of course.'

'Oh, I understand that. But as I told him, in this day and age he couldn't expect the Press not to ask questions and get answers the best and dirtiest way they can. As a matter of fact, we've all been pestered by reporters since Charlotte's death was reported. I told him we were probably having a Press reception to wrap it all up in one go. Obviously we can't comment on the murder. But it would save endless so-called exclusive interviews about Charlotte, what it was like working with her and so on.'

'Do you think that's wise?'

'Not particularly. But it seems to be necessary. Your Inspector Waller wasn't overjoyed, insisted on having a man on hand at the reception. Probably lock us all up when it gets too near the knuckle.' He scratched the deep line that carved a crevice from his cheekbone to the outer edge of a thin good-humoured mouth. 'He wasn't exactly overjoyed either when I told him you were coming to see me.'

Lost for words, Brand decided not to try to find any. He sensed that Ackerman knew this bit of his script precisely and wasn't going to be deflected from it by anything Brand said.

'On the other hand I did detect a note of—how shall I put it?—resignation in his voice. Grumbled something about not being able to stop the old buffer doing what he liked with his spare time provided he didn't interfere with police procedures. Actually I got the impression he rather respected you.'

Good for Waller! Brand relaxed.

'I don't imagine though that I—or anyone else come to that—can tell you anything they haven't already told the police.'

'Facts!'

'You don't put much faith in facts?'

'Not always the facts people present to the police immediately after a crime is committed. You know what everyone's first reaction is when they're confronted by a copper, Mr Ackerman? Innocent or guilty or just a witness: how can I convince him best that I didn't do it? It's totally irrational, mostly unnecessary. But it's a perfectly natural reflex action—these days anyway, when no one trusts the police.'

'So what facts are you questioning?'

Deliberately Brand threw his reply into Ackerman's corner. 'Do you believe the man they have in custody killed Charlotte Saint-Clair?'

'How the hell should I know?' Ackerman began, then stopped. 'It certainly looks that way from what I've heard. But, since you ask, no, I'm not sure I believe he did. And I can't for the life of me think why. It's just something, deep down here.' He stamped a finger on his forehead.

It was that sudden phrase for which Brand had been hoping. Carefully he let it pass, ready to pick it up later. Obviously Ackerman was baffled by his own doubt.

'I suppose it would be absurd to ask if Charlotte Saint-Clair had any . . .'

'. . . enemies? That's a big word. It covers Hitler and the man next door who builds his house too close and blocks out your ancient light.'

'Let's say somewhere in between.'

'In this profession everyone could slaughter everyone else sooner or later. The scriptwriters hate the star when she won't speak the lines they've slaved over. Another player feels she or he has been shabbily treated in favour of the leading lady and naturally they direct their venom at the leading lady.'

'And the producer?'

Ackerman laughed, a good, fruity laugh at his

own expense. 'The producer hates the lot of them until the thing's finished, it's up on the screen and the public loves it. Then everyone loves everyone.'

'What do you know about Joanna Saint-Clair's edgy boyfriend, Russ Gilchrist?'

'Gilchrist,' Ackerman sighed. 'Gilchrist's a pain. If he's turned down for a part he feels as if he's been crucified. I've had to give him the brush-off now and then and he has a fierce temper. Not nice. But then, I suspect you know that.'

It was Brand's turn to chuckle. 'He pulled a gun on me.'

'Well, that's class! He just punched me on the nose.'

'And Charlotte?'

For a moment, Ackerman seemed evasive. He was a straightforward man and he didn't manage it too well. 'Charlotte wasn't in the business of hiring and firing.'

'Not at the end. But earlier?'

'Well, I suppose if I don't tell you you'll dig it out somehow from the cuttings. Years ago when Gilchrist was in his early twenties, that would be nineteen-sixty-something, she was doing a West End revival of *A Streetcar Named Desire*. Perhaps you saw it. Huge success. Of course, she was much too old for Blanche, but she always had that magic, like Edith Evans, she could persuade you she was any age she wanted you to believe. And in her fifties she was still a staggering beauty.'

'I know. I remember.' How he remembered, thought Brand.

'The part of Stanley Kowalski—the one Marlon Brando played on Broadway and on the screen—was up for grabs. They wanted a new young actor, totally a fresh face. As you know, it's a role that can make any actor's name, maybe his career.

'Gilchrist was not long out of RADA,' Ackerman continued. 'He was a likely choice. He'd got the heft, the size. He was an accomplished, though not inspired, actor. But he had potential. To cut a long story short, it came finally to a choice between him and another young actor from RADA. Gilchrist lost out. Unfortunately it was fairly common knowledge that the deciding voice was Charlotte's. To put it unkindly, it was generally thought she rather fancied the other chap. Charlotte's affairs were legion and she wasn't too fussy about the difference in age. Gilchrist couldn't but know that. Apparently there was a godalmighty scene. He swore, rather publicly I fear, to "get her", whatever that meant.'

'And it killed his career or at least his hopes of stardom?'

'It didn't kill anything.. His mediocrity did that. But the other actor went right to the top. Daniel Rosenberg. Great big superstar now,

95

with his own production company, hefty percentage of the profits—gross—pick of all the best roles going. I guess every time Russ Gilchrist reads a line about him in the newspaper, sees him promoting a new film, double page spreads about him in the Sunday Supplements, he thinks: that could have been me.'

'If it weren't for Charlotte Saint-Clair?'

'Maybe. But if I can guess what you're thinking: I don't think he has the makings of a killer either. Could be wrong!'

'So how did it happen that Gilchrist became so friendly with Joanna Saint-Clair? I assume her aunt didn't approve of that relationship.'

'Disapprove is hardly the word. But what could she do? Gilchrist wheedled his way into Joanna's company and, heaven knows why, they liked each other. Maybe loved—or love! No one will ever quite understand Joanna, what she's really thinking. Except perhaps Russ. She was a wonderful companion and secretary and manager and everything else to her aunt. But she kept herself to herself. An enigma, you might say.'

'Did she resent her aunt?'

'As I said. She's an enigma. But if she resented her, she put up with her for an awfully long time. Rather fond of her, myself. Although I don't think she likes me much.'

'I'd appreciate meeting some of your people—

cast, writers, so on. Is that asking too much?' Brand knew it was, but maybe Ackerman didn't.

Ackerman fiddled with the ballpoint on his unusually uncluttered desk.

'I don't imagine they'd mind. My secretary has their phone numbers. I'll tell her to let you have them. But I must speak to them first. In any case I'll let you know when we have our Press reception, if, that is. I think it might amuse you and you can meet them all there. And Gloria Beesley. You've heard of her. Film fan like you. Most feared gossip columnist in Hollywood. She's good for a laugh, too.'

'Mr Ackerman, there's something that perplexes me.'

'Just one thing?'

'One among many. You all seem to be taking this—tragedy, very lightly. Joanna Saint-Clair didn't show any grief. You're making jokes about what will certainly be a ghoulish Press reception. Why?'

'What would you like us to do? Break down and weep all over the front pages? Would that seem proper to you? Would that square with how you think people ought to behave in this situation? Well, show business people aren't ordinary people. Mostly we cry inside. It's better for the image and easier on the ulcers.'

'I take your point.'

'Charlotte was a light. Now that light has

been snuffed out. I care, believe me, Mr Brand, I care. But don't ask me to show it. It's not for public inspection.'

'For the second time today I've been made to feel rather silly.'

'I'm sorry. I know, I sense, your interest in Charlotte is in its way as deeply committed as mine. She meant a lot in your life, didn't she?'

Brand nodded. 'Fans can be very vulnerable, Mr Ackerman.' The conversation was moving into fragile territory which he didn't want invaded—not yet, anyway.

'There is something else,' he said, assuming his authoritative voice again. 'The chain with which she was strangled. It meant a great deal to her. She always wore it. And the clasp—C and L. Would the L stand for Leila Starr?'

Ackerman pondered as if the thought that had been nagging at him earlier was beginning to take shape.

'She never said as much. But I'd always assumed so. I didn't know Charlotte well until after Leila Starr's suicide. And I think it was a painful subject in private, although she talked about Leila quite happily in public.'

'It's just a wild guess, but—was there more than one chain like that?'

'Well, we used a fake in the death scene in *Wild Fortune* because she refused to go through with it if we used the real chain, her chain.'

'Was that unusual? Charlotte Saint-Clair

causing a fuss on the set?'

'Yes, it was, now you come to mention it.'

'You see, if there were two linked letters in the clasp, it's possible, originally, there was another identical chain. Two people plighting their friendship, if you like.'

'I hadn't thought of that,' Ackerman said evasively. But something in his manner suggested that he had and only in the last few minutes.

When Brand had left, Ackerman sat in his chair, watching capricious clouds scudding across the sky, a puzzled frown seaming his weathered face. Then he picked up the phone and asked for Mack Tully.

He cut short Tully's long, frantic dissertation on the organization of the Press reception which had been approved by the directors of Regent TV. 'Mack, I want to look up some old files on Charlotte and Leila Starr. Where's the best source?'

'Information or gossip, rumour and scandal?'

'Gossip, rumour and scandal.'

'Couldn't do better than the *Globe*. And they owe us.'

# CHAPTER TEN

It was almost dark by the time Brand nosed the Subaru across the Surrey-Sussex border and headed towards the coast. The wearing headlights of the oncoming cars reminded him that his eyes were tired and his muscles were aching with fatigue. Although he might look comfortably settled into his sixty-odd years, he seldom felt his age. But tonight he was acutely aware that the hectic hours he'd spent since meeting John Waller at the station that morning were taking their toll physically. What used to be just routine seemed now a breathless obstacle course. It irritated him more than he liked to admit. He wasn't about to let age get the better of him. Not yet. Not for a long time.

And however his body was reacting, his brain remained annoyingly alert. The turn-off to the quiet backwood in the vicinity of Charlotte Saint-Clair's cottage loomed ahead. Almost without thinking, he detoured off the main road. It shouldn't be too difficult to find the pub, The Dragon, where Billy Richards had insisted he'd spent part of the evening in which the murder had been committed. Despite Waller's assurance that the police had followed up all the appropriate leads, he suspected that, in the euphoria of finding such a likely suspect so quickly after the crime, the investigations at the pub had been cursory at least, merely routine at best. He didn't expect to do any better. Waller was no fool. Probably the proprietor would just confirm what he'd already told the police. But it was worth a try. One thing he'd learned during the taxing day was that people tended to confide in a harmless pensioner who posed no threat.

Spotting a local approaching on foot down the hedgerow-lined lane, he stopped the car. The man, about his own age, bundled up in a duffel coal as protection against the unseemly chill of the spring night, looked nervously at the parked car, then, reassured by the sight of Brand as he poked his head out of the passenger seat window, he ambled forward.

Yes, he knew The Dragon. But the beer was better at The Swan. When he realized Brand wasn't interested in the beer, he expressed mild surprise, told him he'd be sorry and gave him complicated instructions, frequently correcting himself, on how to reach The Dragon. 'Mind you,' he said as an afterthought, 'if you go back on the A24, it's the first turning on the left. Can't miss it.'

Well, why the hell didn't you tell me that in the first place, Brand thought irritably. But he thanked him profusely, executed a five point turn in the narrow lane and retraced his journey.

As the man who preferred The Swan had

101

assured him, he couldn't miss it. It was an unprepossessing brick building of little local interest, but the oversize Dragon sign swinging precariously above the saloon bar door was inescapable.

There were only a couple of cars besides Brand's parked outside. Obviously a quiet night. The inside was hardly more welcoming than the exterior, unless the owner believed in cutting down on his electricity bills when trade was sluggish. As Brand entered, the low hum of coversation from the few customers nursing their glasses at stray tables ceased for a moment, then continued just as abruptly. The newcomer was of no interest to them.

Propping himself up at the bar, Brand ordered a pint of bitter, then changed his mind. 'Half,' he said apologetically. This wasn't the time to risk being breathalysed by some eager young copper and he recalled that he'd only eaten half a stale ham sandwich since breakfast. He spotted a tray of sausage rolls. 'Fresh?' he inquired hopefully. The burly man behind the bar looked aggrieved. 'As a daisy,' he said grumpily, plucking a plump one from the tray with his fingers and placing it on a damp plate before Brand.

It wasn't a good beginning.

'Nice little pub,' said Brand agreeably. 'You the manager?'

'Owner,' the man replied, but his tone

seemed more accommodating. He pointed at the sign above the bar: 'Proprietor: E. E. Goodblood.'

'Not much doing tonight?'

'No.' Mr Goodblood surveyed the sparse gathering glumly. 'Always the same, Thursday. Busy early in the week, busy at the end. Thursday, like a morgue around here.'

'Morgue' seemed an appropriate introduction to the purpose of Brand's visit. 'I'd have thought with the murder the other night ... so near ...' He didn't quite know what the murder might have to do with the volume of custom at the pub, but Goodblood responded as he'd hoped.

'You mean that actress? The one who plays Chelsea Fortune?'

He said it casually, as if celebrities were killed every other day in this quiet backwater of Sussex. But Brand sensed a quickening of interest. Mr Goodblood obviously wasn't one to hide his meagre claim to fame under a bushel.

He propped his elbows on the bar and leaned forward. From his breath Brand guessed he wasn't above sampling his own stock on a dull evening. 'Police were round here.'

Brand expressed a gratifying surprise. 'Did she come in here then?' he asked avidly, knowing full well Charlotte Saint-Clair wasn't likely to patronize any pub, let alone one with so little *élan*.

'Well, no,' Goodblood conceded. 'But the chap they caught said he had—on the very night.'

'I didn't know anyone had been charged.'

'Not sure if he's been charged yet. But he's the one who is helping the police with their inquiries. We all know what that means.' He winked broadly. 'Where there's smoke! . . .'

'And what happened?' Brand egged him on, but the proprietor of The Dragon wasn't about to be rushed.

'Came round, bold as brass, the next morning after the body was discovered.' His recital of the facts apparently drew heavily on a study of detective fiction. He paused dramatically. 'Mrs Goodblood and I were just having breakfast. We always believe in a good breakfast, sets you up for the day.'

Brand sighed, but he let him tell his story in his own rambling way.

'Must have given you both a turn,' he sympathized.

'You're not wrong. Never have trouble with the police. Well, just occasionally. Over-running licensing hours. And we get a few tearaways from London, being just off the main road. But nothing important. Nothing I can't deal with—or the Mrs.'

'Anyway,' he went on, 'this chap had told them he'd been here. An alibi, you know,' he said knowledgeably.

'But he hadn't?'

The man shook his head, slightly deflated. It would have made a better story if he could have claimed recognition of Billy Richards.

'Neither Mrs G nor I had seen him. They showed us a photograph. Just a snapshot really. One of his family had given it to them.'

'Blurred? The photograph?'

'Well, you know what happy snaps are like. Could be your Uncle George or your brother Henry. But it was a good enough likeness, I imagine. Anyway we couldn't place him. I mean, you have to be honest, don't you?'

'Absolutely.'

A squat woman, as wide as she was tall, came bustling out of the door that led from the bar to what might have been a kitchen, with another tray of sausage rolls in her hands. She dumped them on the counter. 'And *they'll* be for the birds tomorrow,' she said. 'No one's going to eat them tonight. I told you. But you never listen.'

Her cheery moon face belied the tartness of her manner and tone.

'Very nice,' Brand lied. 'I'll have another.'

'Another bitter, too?' Goodblood asked hopefully.

'Better not, Driving. The law.'

Brand turned his attention to Goodblood's sour companion.

'Mrs Goodblood?' he asked, not needing to be told.

She nodded.

'Your husband's just been telling me about the drama the other day.'

She shot a pained look at her husband who was ineffectually mopping the counter with a none too clean damp cloth. 'He would. Like a tap. Never stops dripping.'

'Come on, Mabel. It's not my fault about the sausage rolls. How was I to know there wouldn't be any customers?'

'I suppose it was a quiet night then, too? When the chap said he was here?'

'No. Actually it wasn't. You remember, Mabel.'

'You don't need to remind me.' She looked even more pained. 'There was a whole mob of them in. Local darts team. They were having a do. A birthday or something.'

'So, there were lots of people around.'

'Rushed off my feet. They can drink, those darts boys. Not like some, she sniffed.

'Did you tell the police that?'

'No, not actually. They didn't really ask. Just wanted to know if we recognized the man in the photograph,' said Goodblood.

'Not that it would have made any difference. I never forget a face,' Mabel asserted primly. She was, thought Brand, exactly the kind of woman who would say she never forgot a face.

'I imagine if you don't have any help it must be pretty wearing when you're busy.'

'Oh, we get help,' said Goodblood. 'Woman comes in twice a week in the evenings, looks after the public bar.' He pointed through the alcove to a drab, unfriendly annexe, now deserted.

'You didn't go into the public bar that night, then?'

'Well, I went in. But mostly we left it to Amy. Never get many people in there. Casuals, in for a quick one and off.'

'Did the police question Amy?'

Goodblood began to look suspicious. Brand's inquiry was becoming too precise for mere curiosity.

'How could they? She wasn't here in the morning, was she?'

Brand, realizing he might have blown his own cover, decided to bluff it out.

'I used to know an Amy. Lived around here. Worked part-time in a pub.' He took a chance. 'Didn't always work here, though, as I recall.'

Goodblood rose to the bait. 'No, she's only been with us for a few months. Used to work at The Swan. Until they got someone full-time.'

The Swan was obviously doing better business than The Dragon.

'That's where I used to see her,' said Brand as if he'd located an old and dear friend. 'Nice woman.'

Mabel sniffed. 'If you like that sort.'

'Lives not far from here, doesn't she?' Brand

probed.

'Just down the lane. "The Willows". Not that there's a willow to be seen. Typical of Amy. It's just a little gatehouse. The big house used to be called "The Willows" and when it was pulled down and developed, Amy kept the name. Sensible people have numbers, not names on their houses.'

Poor Amy, thought Brand. It couldn't be easy being employed, even part-time, by a tyrant like Mabel Goodblood.

'I must look her up some time,' said Brand, finishing his bitter and making it sound like the kind of remark uttered by someone who had no intention of following it through. 'Well, best be getting on.' He appeared as if nothing were further from his mind than a rendezvous with Amy whoever-she-was.

'Far to go?' Goodblood seemed reluctant to let the only lively conversation he'd had that evening end.

'Coast.'

'Well, there's not much chance you'll be had up for drunken driving on the way,' Mabel Goodblood said dismissively.

The crisp night air hit Brand smartly as he let himself out of the dismal pub. It was still only 9.30 pm. With any luck, Amy, with the airs above her station, would be at home.

# CHAPTER ELEVEN

'The Willows' was easy to locate, its ornamental porch flanked by latticed stained-glass windows, disproportionately grand for such a humble dwelling, guarding some stately home that was no longer there.

The woman who answered Brand's knock on the door carried herself with the same fussy dignity as the gatehouse in which she lived. Her small, pointed face and darting eyes gave the impression of a squirrel protecting its hideaway from intruders. She was dressed in a pale blue padded dressing-gown. Although it was buttoned up to the neck, she gripped the collar tightly with tiny, nervous fingers. But her iron grey hair was immaculately dressed in an outdated pompadour style and her make-up looked freshly applied as if, despite the lateness of the hour, she believed in being prepared for any eventuality such as an unexpected caller.

She studied Brand questioningly before asking him the purpose of his business in a voice of painstaking gentility.

'I apologize for bothering you but I was looking for the lady who helps out at The Dragon. It's a matter of some urgency.' Deliberately Brand remained where he was standing, not attempting to move forward until he was invited. He could, after all, hardly have blamed her if she'd slammed the door in his face and told him to return at a respectable hour. But curiosity got the better of any latent timidity.

'Why?' she asked suspiciously.

'It's a police matter,' said Brand with, he hoped, the right blend of reassurance and gravity. He'd decided that an official approach would cause less alarm than a more casual one, even if he could think of one which sounded plausible.

'I'm—I'm assisting the police with their inquiries into the murder of Charlotte Saint-Clair the other night. You probably heard about it,' he continued, uncomfortably aware that if she cared to challenge him he wouldn't have a leg to stand on.

The woman nodded. 'But what's that got to do with me?' she said.

'Then you are Amy . . . ?'

'Amy Winterton. Miss.' She nodded again. She gripped the dressing-gown around her even more tightly. 'I repeat. What's that got to do with me?'

Brand sighed. It wasn't going to be easy. 'Perhaps you'd like to see my credentials,' he volunteered.

He produced his NARPO card, hoping his membership of the National Association of Retired Police Officers would impress her. She peered at it myopically and gave it back to him.

'Retired?' she inquired.

'As I said, I'm assisting the police.' He hoped God and John Waller would forgive him, but he'd worry about that later. For the moment he was more concerned about gaining the confidence of a middle-aged maiden lady in a lonely gatehouse on a country lane. He began to curse the impulse that had made him look for Amy Winterton after leaving The Dragon. If he'd had any sense he'd have left it until the morning when the sudden appearance of a stranger on her doorstep wouldn't have seemed so sinister.

'There are just one or two questions I'd like to ask you. I gather you don't know that the police called on the proprietors of The Dragon, Mr and Mrs Goodblood, yesterday morning?'

'How could I know? I haven't been there for two days. I only work part-time behind the bar, you see. Just as a favour, you understand,' she added quickly. 'I'm used to a better class of occupation. But it brings in a little extra each week. And there's not very much call for my line of work around here. I give piano lessons.'

Her preoccupation with explaining how she came to be involved in anything so demeaning as helping behind the bar in a pub seemed to have taken precedence over her natural suspicion of Brand, even if only temporarily.

'It really is very difficult these days, making ends meet,' she went on, worrying a subject that

111

was obviously never far from her thoughts.

Brand agreed sympathetically.

She pulled herself together, seeming suddenly to take in the incongruity of discussing the rising cost of living on the doorstep late at night with a total stranger.

'What was it you wanted?'

Her tone was slightly warmer.

'Just a couple of questions. I really won't take up much of your time. If you prefer, we can talk here.'

'No, no,' she shivered, 'Come in.'

As she opened the door wider, a plump black Aberdeen terrier waddled lazily through the hall, scrutinized Brand, then turned tail and went off into the rear of the house.

'I'm afraid MacGregor isn't much of a watchdog. He only ever seems to bark at men in uniform—like the postman and the Salvation Army. But as soon as it's dark he shuts up. The vet says he hasn't been trained properly. I expect he's right. But, living out here alone, I wish he were a bit noisier sometimes.'

'Like now?'

'Oh, I didn't mean that.' But clearly she did.

'Miss Winterton, please let me set your mind at rest. All I want is for you to try to remember what happened at The Dragon the night before last?'

'You don't mean Mr and Mrs Goodblood are in any way implicated in that dreadful murder?'

she said.

'Good heavens no. It's just that someone who may be—implicated, that is—could have visited the pub that night. Mr and Mrs Goodblood don't remember. But I understand you tended the public bar that evening.'

She shivered slightly. 'Such a horrible thought! A murderer at The Dragon! Of course, they get some funny customers in there at times. But a murderer!'

'Miss Winterton, you're jumping to conclusions. I didn't say murderer. I just want you to recall, if you can, the people who came into the public bar two nights ago.'

'Well, we weren't very busy. There was quite a party in the saloon bar. The Goodbloods were looking after them. That's why I was in the public. There were some regulars, just popping in.'

'People you know by sight?'

'Oh yes.'

'And no one else?'

'I didn't say that.' When she applied her mind to anything Miss Winterton was obviously very precise. Pity Waller wasted his time on the Goodbloods, thought Brand.

She closed her eyes as if reconstructing the events of the evening.

'There was a sailor who wanted to get to Brighton. He'd taken the wrong turn-off. A young girl—I suspect she was under age, although she didn't look it—and her boyfriend. Rather loud. They insisted on singing noisily, those awful pop songs they like these days. The man in the corner was quite distressed. But, as I told him, they weren't exactly rowdy and anyway there was such a rumpus in the saloon bar, you could hardly complain.'

'Who was the little man in the corner?'

'He came in not long before closing time. I served him a brandy, I think. And he just sat in the corner.'

'As if he were hiding?'

'No, just sitting. Absorbed in whatever he was thinking about, that's why their singing bothered him. He seemed almost in a dream. Well, more of a nightmare. People often come in to drown their troubles. It's not unusual. And I don't invite confidences.'

'He was drowning his troubles?'

'Hardly. On one small brandy.'

'Was there anything unusual about him? Apart from being concerned about the noise?'

'No, I don't believe so. He was quite short, fiftyish, pasty-faced, sort of greyish sandy hair—not much of it.'

Brand recalled Billy Richards standing, small, lost and helpless, in the cell. Amy Winterton's description could have fitted thousands of men. But on that night in that pub, Brand was convinced, it had to be Billy Richards.

'Could you identify that man if necessary,

Miss Winterton?'

At the official-sounding request, she looked alarmed.

'I might. But I couldn't swear.'

'All I'm asking is, if you were asked to identify him in a line-up . . .'

'Of course I would do my duty—however distasteful,' she agreed primly.

'Thank you, Miss Winterton, you've been a great help.'

'Is that all?'

'It's more than enough. You may be instrumental in saving a man from being unjustly charged.' His deliberately pompous assurance seemed to please her.

She patted her nest of grey hair. 'Anything to oblige, Mr . . . ?'

'Brand. Ralph Brand. I used to be a detective-inspector before I retired. By the way, Miss Winterton, I really would see about getting a better watchdog or make sure that MacGregor is properly trained.'

'Perhaps I should,' she conceded. 'But I suspect he's past it.'

As he left 'The Willows' Brand marvelled as he always had at the abstruseness of the general public when faced with a policeman asking questions. It wasn't often a wilful wish to deceive or conceal, sometimes it was just a memory blank which, with endless, patient questioning, could be unlocked. But it took time and time wasn't always on the side of the investigating officer.

If only the Goodbloods had remembered to tell Waller that Amy Winterton had been serving in the public bar on the night Charlotte Saint-Clair had been murdered, maybe Billy Richards wouldn't have been such an easy suspect. It didn't prove that he couldn't have killed Charlotte, but it did show that he wasn't lying about his whereabouts. At least, it was a snip of evidence that should be passed on to Waller. The evening paper hadn't carried the news that a man had been charged, so perhaps the Chief Constable had also decided that the Superintendent and Waller were being a bit previous.

At the call-box on the corner of the main road, Brand phoned the station. Waller was still there. From the tone of his voice Brand gathered he hadn't had a peaceful day either.

'I hear you've been putting yourself about, Ralph.' He sounded edgy and unwelcoming. 'I'm warning you, if we get one complaint about a retired police officer taking upon himself more authority than he has, there'll be trouble. More to the point, *I'll* be in trouble.'

Brand shut him up smartly. 'You haven't charged him?'

'Not yet. Chief Constable thinks we should have something harder to go on.'

'You can't hold him much longer.'

'You don't have to tell me that. The family solicitor has made that very plain. We're releasing him. No option.'

'I may have something for you.'

He sensed John Waller snapping to attention and took his time telling him about Amy Winterton and her little man in the public bar.

'Why the blazes didn't the Goodbloods tell us there was someone else serving there that night?' Waller fumed when Brand had finished. 'Not that it's much,' he went on grudgingly, 'she said he was in a state, didn't she? Which could mean he'd actually killed Saint-Clair. The timing's right.'

'It could also mean that he saw her dead body and in a state of shock went to the pub, drank a brandy, then went back to the lane by her cottage where he was found. And if he was in a state of shock it would explain why you can't get much sense out of him.'

'Oh Christ, you and your theories, Ralph! Anyway, she has to identify him first. I'll get on to it first thing in the morning. And, Ralph, thanks. You haven't lost your touch.'

'Old coppers never do. And, incidentally, you might run a check on whether a chap named Russ Gilchrist has a licence to own a firearm. He's Joanna Saint-Clair's boyfriend, actor, and he has a nasty habit of waving it around when he's angry.'

'How the hell . . . ?'

'Sorry, John. No more ten pence. I'll keep in touch.'

He heard John Waller plaintively calling 'Where are you?' before the phone went dead on him.

His spirits were buoyant after his chat with Waller. The weariness he'd felt earlier had drained out of him. And the full moon that now transformed the trees and hedgerows into silvery phantoms seemed to beckon him on. The long day wasn't over yet.

With renewed vigour Ralph Brand drove off the main road again, this time in the direction of Charlotte Saint-Clair's cottage.

## CHAPTER TWELVE

She'd always called it her secret retreat. But there had never been anything very secret about Charlotte Saint-Clair's cottage in the country. Even her cosy definition of it as a 'cottage' was a fantasy that suited her whim when she bought it twenty years before. It was in fact a handsome folly built by the Prince Regent for one of his minor mistresses, renovated and enlarged by subsequent owners, set in a prettily landscaped old English garden. From the outside the white-walled house looked smaller than it actually was, preserving a cottagey image without the inconvenience of tiny windows and low ceilings that went with living in a cottage. A couple from the neighbouring village lovingly tended the garden and kept the house in order when Charlotte was away, which was often. She didn't care for living-in servants although a previous resident had built a flat over the garage.

It had been featured often in glossy monthlies as a background to gracious photographs of Charlotte decoratively posing with secateurs in the rose-garden or draped across the chaise-longue in a floating tea-gown in the sitting-room. The locals were rather proud of having a celebrity for a neighbour, though they affected not to be impressed in their close Sussex fashion.

So public was her private life that any mildly interested reader of the magazines or gossip columns could easily locate where Charlotte Saint-Clair lived when, as she put it, she wanted 'to get away from it all'. Except, of course, like many stars with outsize egos, she brought it with her. There were the weekend parties attended by famous names from the theatre, television and the cinema; the entourage of visitors who just 'dropped in' because they knew they'd always be welcome.

Except, thought Brand, on the night of her death when for some reason she'd preferred to be alone, watching her own demise on television, perhaps relishing the effect it was having on millions of viewers. As he turned into the lane fronting the wrought-iron gate he noticed a patrol car parked a few yards ahead.

It was too late for sightseers, too quiet for reporters and the boys from the forensic laboratory would have done their work. The patrol car was a token advertisement that the law was on hand to keep an eye on the property and scare off any untoward intruders. Brand had no doubt that he'd been spotted. Before he'd switched off the engine a chunky uniformed policeman had got out of the patrol car and was peering at Brand through the windscreen of the Subaru.

'Might I inquire what you're doing here, sir?' he said politely but firmly. In the light of the full moon Brand could see the questioning expression crease into a warm smile. 'Why, it's Inspector Brand, isn't it?'

'That's right. Only not Inspector any more. Retired.'

'Rawlings. You remember me.'

Brand did indeed. He'd hoped that he would know the coppers on duty and luck had been on his side. Rawlings had been a green recruit fresh from training school when he'd joined the Sussex constabulary. He'd been suitably in awe of the Inspector whose bark was invariably worse than his bite as he had had good reason to learn during his first week on the Force. Instead of bawling him out for an error of judgement

Brand had sensed his insecurity, taken the trouble to set him right and then joined him for a pint in the local. After that they'd strictly observed the rules of rank. But he'd always had a soft spot for Brand, whatever the others might say.

'Nice to see you, Rawlings. How are things?'

The pleasant face made a grimace. 'Pretty dull. All the excitement's over. Here anyway. Just routine surveillance. What brings you here, sir?'

'I was talking to Inspector Waller about the case this morning. I just thought as I was passing...' He left the request hanging in mid-air.

'Sorry, sir, I've orders not to let anyone in without permission.'

'Well, you know me, Rawlings.'

Another younger uniformed figure loomed into view.

'What's the trouble, Tom?' He was new to Brand. No shared memories there.

'No trouble. It's Inspector Brand. Used to be. You know.'

'Only by reputation.' The other man looked dubious, betraying the impatience of youth with old coppers who couldn't leave the job alone.

'He just wants to take a look at the house.' Rawlings made it sound as casual and natural as he could out of deference to Brand, but his companion was having none of that.

'Orders,' he said abruptly, shaking his head.

'Quite right,' agreed Brand. 'Look, why not get on the blower to Inspector Waller? I've just spoken to him on the phone. He's probably still at the station.'

The two men exchanged silent questions and agreed an answer.

'All right,' the keen young one said grudgingly.

As Rawlings went back to the patrol car, his partner leaned closer to the windscreen studying Brand as if he were some useless relic from the past. As was his wont in an awkward situation, Brand took out his pipe and seemed absorbed in filling and lighting it, shrewdly using the silence to defuse the aggravation. It was a game he was adept at playing. As he'd judged, he could hold out longer than the young copper.

Finally, the man spoke. 'What's the interest?'

'Curiosity.'

'Nothing much to see. It's all locked up.'

'Then I can't do any harm, can I?'

'I didn't mean that, sir.' The young man sounded faintly embarrassed. The respectful 'sir' was a giveaway.

'I know you didn't,' said Brand, realizing he'd won the silent sparring match and not wishing to prolong it.

He heard Rawlings crunch up the lane towards them.

'Inspector Waller said you could take a look,

122

but only a few minutes, sir. It's—well, irregular, you know.'

'I'll bet that's not all he said,' Brand chuckled, as he lumbered out of the car.

'Not exactly.' Now it was Rawlings's turn to sound embarrassed. 'There was quite a bit more, but he said he owed you.' Brand knew it was on the tip of his tongue to ask exactly what Waller owed his old Inspector. But Brand wasn't inclined to elaborate.

As he opened the wrought-iron gate and trudged up the path to Charlotte Saint-Clair's cottage, the two policemen watched his retreating figure.

'Beats me,' said the younger one. 'What the hell can he expect to get out of looking round the outside of an old house in the moonlight?'

Rawlings smiled, remembering. 'He's sniffing the atmosphere.'

'What's that supposed to mean?'

'Getting the feel of the place where a murder was committed. That's what he always used to say when he was on the Force. Follow your instinct, follow your nose. There's more to detecting than matching fingerprints and blood types. It paid off, too.'

'If he was such a bloody good detective why didn't he ever make Super or Chief?'

Rawlings thought for a moment. 'Perhaps because he never learned that in the police force rules aren't made to be broken.'

The young one took off his cap and scratched his head. 'You've lost me.' They walked back to their watching post in the patrol car until Brand's few minutes was up.

Outlined in the bright moonlight the house was instantly recognizable from the many photographs of it Brand had seen in the magazines. He circled round its circumference imagining Charlotte Saint-Clair living there. No, not living there. Gracing it with her presence. Even at night it wasn't forbidding. It gave off no aura of loneliness. It wasn't a house in which a person on her own would be prey to irrational fears, a creak on the stairs, a rustling in the loft, a footstep in the hall. A friendly home.

On the night she died, Charlotte Saint-Clair would have felt comfortable in her security, heedless of the night sounds of an old house, Brand judged.

The cloying scent of early wallflowers, ranked in borders beside the path, attacked his nostrils as he stood facing the front door. From force of habit he tried the handle. Surprisingly, he felt a click as the door gave way, opening out on to a finely proportioned hall.

Someone hadn't done their job properly, thought Brand with the rising annoyance of a trained officer confronted by an indication of inexcusable negligence. He made a half-hearted turn to call Rawlings to account. But the temptation to enter the house so invitingly open to him was too great. He'd leave the reprimand he was no longer qualified to administer till later.

The house seemed to be beckoning him on as he opened downstairs doors with gloved hands, taking in the lay-out of the rooms: a charming sitting-room, serviceable dining-room, a trophy-lined study, a large lounge stuffed with easy chairs and Heal's sofas, an ample country kitchen and scullery. Nothing there but the material evidence of a well ordered life-style.

His footsteps muffled by the thick carpeting he climbed the stairs to the floor above. He thought he heard the sound of rustling papers. It was merely momentary. And then total silence, the unnatural silence of someone holding their breath.

He waited poised on the staircase. Reason told him not to proceed. To walk smartly out of the house and call Rawlings. But, against all his better judgement, he remained rooted to the spot. It was as if the house were willing him to stay, as if Charlotte Saint-Clair were still exercising the same hold she'd had over him during her life on the stage and in her films.

The silence ticked the seconds away, but still Brand waited. After what must have been a full two minutes, he cautiously continued to the top of the stairs. There was no sign of another presence. Perhaps, after all, it had been just a mouse in the rafters, a loose window-latch.

Half a dozen firmly shut doors led off the wide, L-shaped upper hall, but another in the corner of the angle was ajar. Brand pushed it open. As it swung back noiselessly it revealed a surprisingly spacious rooom, probably a master bedroom, with large windows on two sides overlooking the rose-garden. But it wasn't the windows or the rose-garden that caught Brand's eye. It was the white chalked outline on the mink-coloured carpet of a figure contorted in the grotesque shape of sudden death. This was where Charlotte Saint-Clair had lain, strangled by her own gold chain two nights ago. The clinical chalk marks were all that remained in this house of the vibrant life which had inhabited it. The possessions were inconsequential. The chalk marks were the reality.

Brand felt an uncomfortable lump aching in his throat as he stood transfixed before the outline of Charlotte's corpse. Without thinking, he reached for a handkerchief in his pocket and blew his nose noisily.

Deliberately he turned aside, shutting that grim outline out of his line of vision. He was about to leave the room when he noticed a Victorian bureau squatting beside the wall behind the door. The roll top was open, a scattering of papers on the desk. He picked them up idly. Bills, receipts, letters, agreements. There was something wrong. The police would never have left the bureau in this mess after they'd done their work.

He peered closer, the bright moonlight from the window over his shoulder giving him an eerily clear vision. Hidden behind the sturdy layer of drawers on the right of the desk he saw what he suspected would be there. The traditional secret drawer that Victorian cabinet-makers invariably introduced into their designs. It was half open, an envelope spilling out of it had obviously been hastily torn apart. From the impression left on the outside it seemed to have contained something heavy. But there was something else which had either been overlooked or perhaps forgotten.

It was a slip of flimsy notepaper, the kind used for air letters. The handwriting was firm and positive, well spaced, as if the writer had wanted to place the maximum emphasis on every word. He barely needed his ever handy pencil torch to read it.

The message was curt with no date, no indication to whom it was addressed. *'Now that she's dead I thought she'd want you to have this—to remember her by!!! I hope it gives you nightmares. She's beyond caring. But I won't let the boy forget!'* It was signed with an initial: 'E'.

Before he had time to re-read the note, Brand felt a crawling sensation at the back of his neck. He'd experienced it often before. It was allied to

127

no sound, no action. It was the suspended moment of approaching threat. He turned swiftly but too late.

An agonizing pain shot through his scalp, his eyes blurred, a dizzying scream seemed to echo through his head, pounding at his brain. He was aware of some astringent fragrance—sandalwood, perhaps. Then there was a black nothing.

When he came to he was slumped on the floor, his head felt as if it had been through a meat-grinder. He lay there for a few moments, waiting for the shock to subside. Gradually his vision cleared, though the back of his head continued to throb with pain. Gripping the sides of the bureau he levered himself up, tested his legs and found, thankfully, that they did as he directed them.

He couldn't have been out for more than five minutes or so, but time enough for his assailant to get away. Still, maybe he was in the grounds, somewhere. The note he'd discovered in the bureau had disappeared, but then he'd hardly expected otherwise.

Stumbling down the stairs and out of the house, he called hoarsely for Rawlings. He heard two pairs of footsteps running up the drive. 'What bloody kind of surveillance is this? Some bugger got in and got me,' he barked, before passing out again into the sickly aroma of wallflowers.

128

# CHAPTER THIRTEEN

The police surgeon who had been summoned from his bed to the station, protesting but resigned, grumpily examined the bump on Brand's head and tested his eyesight, heartbeat and balance. His touch was none too tender.

'What's an old codger like you doing fooling around the scene of the crime alone at night? You ought to know better.'

He rolled down his sleeves. 'You'll survive. But I suppose we should take an X-ray. Although it would probably only prove that you've got a screw loose. Lucky you turned just when you did. Otherwise he'd have clobbered you square and you wouldn't be wasting my beauty sleep here, you'd be laid out unconscious on a hospital bed—or worse.'

He looked over Brand's head at John Waller and his sergeant. His expression was more grave than his lightly insulting commentary on Brand's condition suggested.

'Right, Ralph. Don't forget to check in for that X-ray tomorrow. Christ! It's tomorrow now. And do me a favour, don't fall down a manhole as you go home.'

He snapped his bag shut, grunted good-night at the three men and left.

'Cheerful bugger, isn't he?' said Brand,

managing a grin.

'He just doesn't suffer fools gladly. Any more than I do,' Waller replied, but the concern in his voice took the edge off the criticism of Brand's unorthodox expedition to Charlotte Saint-Clair's cottage.

Brand waved aside the derisive remark. 'I don't know. Maybe my bump on the head has done you layabouts a favour. Whoever thumped me it certainly couldn't have been Billy Richards. They also had a key to the front door and they knew that something possibly incriminating was hidden in the bureau. So whoever murdered Chelsea—I mean Charlotte—' he tapped his sore head and winced, partly at the pain and partly at the irritating tendency to confuse the actress with the part she'd played on TV—'whoever murdered Charlotte wasn't a stray passer-by, but someone who knew her intimately.'

'We're checking all that. By the way, thanks for the tip about Gilchrist. In fact, you'll be surprised to know, Ralph, we've been checking on all her intimates and associates since the body was discovered.' Waller's heavy sarcasm wasn't lost on Brand.

'I'm sorry, John. Getting a bit above myself,' he conceded. 'But you have to admit . . .'

Waller raised his hands above his head, anticipating the argument. 'I know. The boys on the spot were lax. They'll be reprimanded.

130

But you've seen the location. Wooded area. Not difficult for anyone to slip in unnoticed.'

'Go easy on them. Rawlings. Good bloke. Natural mistake,' said Brand quickly, remembering what it was like to be on the sharp end of a reprimand. 'Did they find any traces?'

'Nothing.' Waller shook his head. 'By the time they'd got to you the chap—or woman—had got clear away. He could even have had a bicycle stashed in the bushes.'

'You said "woman".'

'Well, it's not beyond the bounds. Women can wield blunt instruments as lethally as men.'

'And what about the note? *"Now that she's dead I thought she'd want you to have this. I hope it gives you nightmares. I won't let the boy forget."* I'm not so cockeyed that I don't remember what it said.'

'I'm not questioning your memory, Ralph. But we've only your say-so. The note's gone. Evidence, Ralph, *evidence!*' He spoke with the exasperation of a parent chiding a stubborn child, the tone Waller now invariably used on his former superior.

Brand affected not to hear the warning note. 'It was signed "E". Think about that, John. "E".'

'There are probably dozens of "E's" in Charlotte Saint-Clair's past. Or present. Errol Flynn, Edward G Robinson, Edith Evans, Duke Ellington—she was a big jazz fan, did you know that? Elaine Pelham in her own TV show. But it's all hypothetical until we recover the note and whatever it was *you* think must have been in the envelope.'

Brand frowned, though the effort caused him more pain. His head still felt like one of Muhammad Ali's used punching-bags. 'It's there. Staring us in the face. In the past. If you turn up anything—anything—John, you'll let me know? I'm entitled.'

Waller nodded.

'Particularly from the States.'

'Of America?' Waller's sergeant, who'd observed the scene between the two men with some amusement, uttered for the first time.

'Where else? That note was written on air letter paper, I could swear.'

Waller walked slowly across the room, clamped his hands on the arms of the chair Brand was occupying and leaned forward. 'Ralph! Give up. *Please.* I can't order you. I can only ask. And I'm asking.'

'And I'm not listening, John. Some sod gave me this—' he pointed to his head.

'Leave it to us. Ralph, can't you understand what I'm trying not to spell out?'

'Of course I understand. I'm not that far gone. I'm getting in too deep. I'm getting too close. Someone thinks I'm a threat. That's about the size of it, isn't it?'

'And the next time you may not be so lucky.

You're an infuriating swine, but I don't want to attend your funeral yet.'

Brand smiled at his former sergeant. 'I know it's in my best interests, John. Not just because I'm making a nuisance of myself. But you know me, when I get the bit between the teeth. Besides, I'm a survivor. A cockroach. That's what someone once told me, not kindly meant, I might add. After Hiroshima, did you know, cockroaches were the first form of life to emerge intact? That's a bit of useless information for free.'

'Don't change the subject. If I can't persuade you. Or the Super. Or the Chief Constable. How about Superintendent Buller?' He paused, waiting for the name to sink in.

Brand chuckled. 'Josh Buller!'

'That's right. Our lords and masters have decided in their out-dated wisdom it might be useful to call on the services of Scotland Yard.'

&ast; &ast; &ast;

'Well, I'll be damned. Josh Buller! He was a rookie on the beat when I was a station sergeant in Streatham. Ornery devil, but a good policeman. One of the best. So, I'll have a friend at court.'

'You've lots of friends, Ralph. But think about it. If you persist, you'll have no official back-up, no squad cars to call on, like in the old

133

days. You'll be on your own.'

'We're all on our own, John. When it comes to the final crunch. Have you done with me? For now?'

Waller sighed. 'Sleep on it, Ralph. Do you want someone to drive you home?'

'No. I'm OK.'

'How do you feel?'

'Fine. Lousy, actually. But I will be fine.'

'By the way, I almost forgot. We had a call for you from Sam Ackerman, the producer of the TV show. Seems you must have made quite an impression on him. He said the Press reception has been fixed for seven tomorrow—tonight—at the Regent TV offices, the boardroom. He particularly, urgently, as I remember, wanted you to go. You won't, I hope. I wish to blazes it wasn't taking place. But we've no authority to stop it. Anyway we'll keep an eye on it. Couple of our chaps mingling with the vultures from the Press and their prey.'

'Interesting,' said Brand, feeling surprisingly chipper again, despite his injury. There was nothing like the scent of a new development to get the adrenalin working. He eased himself out of his chair, nodded to the sergeant and winked at John. 'See you, chummy.'

'Get off with you, knuckle-head.'

'I love you, too.' Brand tipped the hat he wasn't wearing in a cheeky salute.

Knowing Waller was watching him intently as

he took off down the corridor, he assumed a jaunty swagger which he managed to sustain until he was out on the pavement and out of sight.

Waller perched on the edge of his desk, tapping his teeth with a ballpoint pen. 'Doesn't change, does he?' said his sergeant. Bob Essex had been working with Waller since the latter's promotion and, though he didn't realize it, their relationship was easing into the same mould as the one enjoyed previously by Brand and Waller: a friendly armed truce of mutual respect and occasional fierce differences.

'No, he doesn't. He won't see reason, you know. Stubborn as they make 'em. Well, you know what to do. Get on to it. But, softly, softly, mind. He may act foolishly at times, but he's no fool. Let's call it a night—what there is of it. I've about had it.'

'Which leaves me holding the baby,' Essex groaned. He thought of his own young wife and baby whom he'd barely seen in the last forty-eight hours.

'Goes with the job, laddie,' said Waller, sounding just like Brand.

★　　★　　★

Brand awakened to a reproachful spring morning, too overcast to promise sunshine but not forbidding enough to encourage sloth. His head throbbed as he lifted it from the pillow. Perhaps, he thought, as he allowed the pain to ease off into a manageable dull ache, I am getting too old for this game. Then he realized that the noises in his head weren't all emanating from the bump he'd received the night before. The telephone by his bedside was ringing insistently. He tried to ignore it, but the caller obviously wasn't going to give up easily.

'Mr Brand?' He recognized the voice at the other end instantly and sat up too jerkily for comfort. He shut his eyes tightly until the sudden shooting pain behind his forehead had run its course.

'Mr Brand?'

'That's me,' he croaked.

'Are you all right? You don't sound to good.' The voice obviously didn't acknowledge the need to identify itself.

'I don't feel too good either, Miss Saint-Clair.' He sensed his brain clearing as he eased himself out of bed and blessed his sturdy constitution. 'Someone conked me on the head when I went to your aunt's cottage last night.' All his old alertness returned as he waited for her reaction.

'You were there?'

'Well, I wasn't at Buckingham Palace,' he said irritably.

'I'm sorry, I just didn't realize...' Her voice trailed away, then returned, apologetic yet guarded. 'Do you have any idea who did it? I thought the house was shut up. Policemen outside.'

Brand weighed the receiver in his hand for a few moments. He was taking a risk, but in for a penny, in for a pound. 'I've a pretty good idea.'

She didn't ask him to elaborate, whether from caution or knowledge he couldn't tell.

'Mr Brand, I telephoned because I wondered...' She seemed to be having difficulty saying what she wanted to say. 'I wondered whether you could find time to see me. It really is quite important. We could talk on the phone, but I'd rather not.'

It was a switch Brand hadn't anticipated. The sharp, cool, efficient woman, who'd managed to make him feel rather like a cuddly old buffer at their previous meeting, was begging for assistance. First Ackerman, now Joanna Saint-Clair. Somewhere along the line he'd done something right.

'Of course I'd be glad to meet you. But if it's something important, don't you think you should tell the police? After all, as you know, I'm retired. I don't rate.' He was ragging her gently, enjoying the satisfaction of turning the tables.

'Frankly, Mr Brand, I wouldn't know where to begin with the police. You see, I don't think—at least I hope—it has anything to do with the murder. I just need to tell someone who's in a position to advise me, someone I can trust. I think I can trust you, Mr Brand.'

'Advise you about what?'

'Please!'

'All right. Mr Ackerman's asked me to attend the Press reception they're giving at Regent TV later today . . .'

'Well, that's fine. I promised to go, too. I didn't want to. But as Mack Tully explained, he's the publicity man, I'd just be pestered constantly by reporters otherwise. And it was a way of getting it over in one go. Not that they'd be much interested in me.'

'I wouldn't be too sure of that. Next of kin?'

'You don't have to remind me. These last couple of days have been a living nightmare.'

'That's not the impression you gave me yesterday, Miss Saint-Clair.'

'Oh, for Pete's sake, call me Joanna or Jo. Miss Saint-Clair sounds like an appendage of the deceased. And, Mr Brand, I thought policemen didn't go by first impressions. We all put on faces, you know.'

Brand smiled to himself. Smart lady! That had been his first impression and she hadn't yet given him cause to change it. Joanna Saint-Clair wanted something, badly enough to humble herself in asking for his help.

'Then we could meet at the reception.'

'No, that wouldn't be private enough. Look, I'm going to the cottage to collect some things. Inspector Waller knows. It's not far from you. I

138

could pick you up this afternoon and drive you to London. I just need to drop into the flat in Kensington when I get there and we could go on together to the shindig.'

Normally Brand preferred to drive himself, at his own pace, with his own thoughts. But his aching head reminded him he didn't feel up to the journey alone and he could always book in somewhere cheap and cheerful like the Grosvenor at Victoria for the night.

'That sounds sensible,' Brand agreed.

She didn't immediately reply, but he thought he heard her sigh of relief.

'And by the way, Miss Saint-Clair—sorry, Joanna—how did you know where I lived?'

'Easy. I looked it up in the phone book.'

She sounded more in control of herself, needling him in that amiable, amused fashion he remembered. There was a 'mission accomplished' tone in her voice as she bade him *au revoir* until later.

He showered, shaved, examined the damage from the night before, decided it was on the mend and felt up to cooking himself a hearty breakfast. To hell with X-rays, he thought. All the same, a judicious call to Waller seemed prudent. One bump on the head was a misfortune. Two would be carelessness.

# CHAPTER FOURTEEN

She didn't talk much on the journey to London, except for polite trivia about the prettiness of the countryside and the inclemency of the weather. When she'd collected him, she'd expressed formal regret at his accident, as she termed it, but didn't dwell on it, as if it were some unfortunate incident that was no concern of hers. She'd refused his offer of tea or coffee, surveyed his small, scrupulously tidy and rather anonymous flat dismissively and insisted she wanted to be on the road as soon as possible. Joanna Saint-Clair hardly seemed the same person who had plaintively asked for his advice only a few hours before.

Brand was thankful for her silence. It gave him the chance to study the woman at the wheel, as he shifted his bulk from one uncomfortable position to another in the passenger seat. Minis weren't made for fleshy, ageing men, he thought ruefully.

She drove as efficiently as she seemed to conduct her life, swiftly but within the speed limits, 'reading' the road carefully as too few drivers did these days. She was wearing a green silk scarf wound turban-style round her head and a good heather tweed suit, immaculately cut but dated, as if it had walked out of a Harrods' advertisement of twenty-five years ago. On her it looked interesting, not for what it revealed but for what it concealed. She wore her clothes like a disguise, part of some masquerade that he found intriguing.

As they approached the busy inner suburbs of London even the courtesies of polite conversation stopped, although she allowed herself the occasional mumbled curse at larger, speedier cars cutting carelessly into her lane. At least, thought Brand, it proved she was human.

When they reached Kensington High Street she neatly manoeuvred the Mini into the only vacant residents' parking space outside the block of flats where her aunt had lived in town, narrowly beating a Rover with CD plates and a glowering uniformed driver.

As she turned off the ignition she sighed. 'I think,' she said, 'we could both do with a drink, don't you?' Then noting Brand's raised eyebrows, she added, 'A tea-time drink to set us up for this evening.'

The porter nodded gravely, made some awkward expression of sympathy and seemed ready to launch into a soliloquy about the virtues of that great lady who had been so cruelly done to death, before Joanna cut him short. 'I know how you feel, Mr Bates, we're all shocked.'

'It's the reporters I can't stand,' he persisted, although clearly he'd been enjoying every

141

minute of the sudden drama which had erupted into the humdrum routine of his job.

'I'm sure you handled the situation magnificently, Mr Bates,' she assured him graciously, then to Brand: 'Mr Bates is a rock, always a great help to my aunt.'

The elderly man turned pink with pleasure. 'It's been my privilege, Miss Saint-Clair.' Brand smiled, again admiringly. Joanna Saint-Clair had a knack of coping with every occasion.

As he entered the spacious flat on the fourth floor, he sensed the presence of Charlotte Saint-Clair instantly. Pausing on the threshold, he breathed it in as if it were some potent perfume with mystical properties. Strange that this should be the closest he would ever get to the woman he'd revered for so many years.

He was suddenly aware that Joanna Saint-Clair was looking at him with that tantalizing, amused expression. 'You're allowed to come in,' she said mockingly.

'It's very nice,' he said inadequately. 'Nice' was a lame description for this, for him, holy of holies.

'Whisky, gin, sherry?'

'A beer would be better.'

'I'll see.' She went off to the kitchen and he used her absence to wander round the elegantly furnished sitting-room, examining the trophies of Charlotte's past—the small Picasso, the signed photographs of the famous, the bits and pieces, some priceless, some merely of sentimental value that she'd picked up on her travels.

When she returned with a can of lager and a glass in her hands, he was studying the portrait over the mantelpiece.

'Sorry, best I could do.'

'Lager will be fine.'

'What do you think of it?' she said lightly, indicating the painting.

'It's probably a decent likeness,' he conceded, standing back. 'But not a good portrait. Perhaps that's as it should be. If it were good it would be overpowering.'

'I know what you mean. One Charlotte in the flesh was more than enough.'

She poured herself a small gin with a lot of tonic and settled herself on the settee. 'Make yourself comfortable,' she urged him. 'It's only five-thirty. We don't have to be at that wretched reception until after seven.' It was as if she were telling him: I'm in control here. Well, we'll see, thought Brand, as he picked the most comfortable armchair in the room and levered himself into it.

'How's your head?' she asked casually.

He really hadn't thought about it since she'd picked him up at his flat, but now that she mentioned it he realized that the pain, though still persistent, was subsiding.

'Manageable,' he replied. He sipped the lager

with some distaste. Then he placed it symmetrically on the coaster she'd provided. 'Is this all you wanted to see me for, pleasant chit-chat, Miss Saint-Clair?'

'Joanna.'

'Joanna, Jo, Miss Saint-Clair. Don't fudge around. I've accepted your invitation, now I want to know what you're inviting me for,' he exploded, though the effort reminded the pain in his head to assert itself. She cupped her glass in her hands, swivelling it gently from left to right. 'Russ has disappeared. Russ Gilchrist,' she whispered.

'What do you mean? Disappeared?'

'Just that. He took off after you left yesterday. Said he was going after some job, an audition. I didn't believe him. I know there's nothing in the offing at the moment. That is, if anyone would employ him anyway. But I let him think I believed him. I thought he'd turn up, probably a bit drunk, later.'

'And he didn't?'

'No. I waited at that awful little hovel for several hours. Then I decided I couldn't hang around any longer. I left a note for him. I checked in at a little hotel not far away. I couldn't stand coming back here alone and I certainly didn't want to spend the night at the cottage, Charlotte's place. You can understand that?'

Brand nodded. 'Is there anywhere he could

have been?'

'I phoned everywhere. His friends. He shares a dump with some other actor in London. He hadn't seen him for several days. He didn't contact me at the hotel. And when I went round to that place he'd rented in the village—where you saw us—this morning, he hadn't been back there either.'

'And the gun? The pistol?'

She took a deep breath. 'That had gone too. Mr Brand, I'm worried about him. He's, well, you saw for yourself—unstable. He doesn't mean to do crazy things, but he does. He can't seem to help it.'

'Why do you put up with him?'

She smiled, a deprecating smile as if the laugh was on her. 'I sometimes wonder. Perhaps because he was so unlike Charlotte. Oh, I was very useful to her, managing the odds and ends of her life and her career. I don't underestimate myself. But she never needed me, really needed me. Charlotte only needed Charlotte. But Russ needed *me*. I think I was a sort of life support for him. And in a funny kind of way—how can I put it?—he *completed* me. I'm not in love with him, you know—except perhaps as a mother loves a difficult child more than the reasonable ones. That's why I appreciated the way you handled him yesterday, sympathetically. Most people just treat him as a damned nuisance. And if enough people think you're a damned nuisance you begin to believe that's all you are.'

She was staring deeply, intently, into her glass as if she could find there some kind of reassurance or comfort.

'Joanna, you must know that Gilchrist had a great grudge against your aunt?' Brand said gently.

'I suppose Sam Ackerman told you that.' She sat back and rested her head wearily on the cushioned back of the settee. 'Of course I knew. He went on about it incessantly. How she'd prevented him from becoming a great star.' She gave a hollow laugh with no mirth in it. 'A great star! Poor Russ, he never stood an earthly. He just didn't have what it took. He hadn't the drive, the charisma, even the talent. Oh, he wasn't a bad actor. But he could never have been anything but a third-rater.'

She pulled herself up abruptly. 'Funny. I'm talking about him as if he were dead. Well, so far as his career was concerned, he was dead a long time ago.'

'Did he ever make threats against your aunt?'

'Constantly. But he'd make threats against anyone who crossed him.'

'How did you come to meet him?'

'Some party or other. At first I thought he just wanted to get to know me because of Charlotte. Then when I realized how he felt about her, I still thought his interest in me was because of her. But later I knew it wasn't like that. I think maybe I was one of the few people who ever bothered to listen to him, let him pour out his troubles.'

'Joanna, I don't quite know how to put this. But has it occurred to you that you might be in danger?'

'From Russ? Really...'

'No, seriously. After last night and what happened to me at the cottage, it's pretty certain that the man the police were questioning didn't murder your aunt. He was just in the right place at the wrong time. Coincidence.'

'So it could be any one of us who knew her well?'

'And hated her. There doesn't seem to be any question that Gilchrist hated her. If in one of those mad moments of his he did strangle her, the person most likely to suspect would be you, because you know him well, know his movements. This is all guesswork, of course. But you could be, let's just say, vulnerable.'

The distress in her eyes was unmistakable, whether from Brand's warning or fear for Gilchrist, he couldn't be sure.

'That's what John Arthur keeps telling me. One of the two main scriptwriters on the TV show, you know.'

'I've heard of him.'

'John's a good friend, an ally you might say in dealing with Charlotte. Rather touchingly, he seemed concerned about my relationship with

Russ. He knew him of old and warned me that at times he wasn't responsible for his actions—nice way of putting it.'

'Maybe you should have taken heed of John Arthur's warning.'

'Before it got to this stage?'

'Well, too late for that. But with Gilchrist on the loose, you can't be too careful. I think you should let Inspector Waller know that Gilchrist has gone missing. Tell him all you know. He could give you some protection.'

'No.' She cut him short angrily. 'No. I can't. Don't you see? Poor bastard's had the short end of the deal all his life, I can't just turn the police loose on him because he's taken off for a couple of days.'

'That's not the way you told it to me.'

'Because I *trusted* you, Mr Brand. I don't believe for a moment that Russ would harm me. He's not like that with me. Oh God, I don't know why I wanted to explain all this to you. It doesn't do any good.'

'It might. If you took my advice. That's what you asked for.'

'Well, I'm not taking it. Not yet anyway.'

'Then the most I can say is, have a care. Stay at the flat here where there's some kind of protection, the porter, an entryphone. And don't see him if he turns up unless someone else is with you. If you won't tell the police, tell your friend, John Arthur.'

148

'All right. I promise that.'

She stood up and smoothed the wrinkles out of her skirt. 'I suppose we should think about making our way to Regent Street.'

'Just a moment. Now there's something I'd like to ask you and I'd appreciate the truth. You haven't wondered what I was doing at your aunt's cottage last night.'

'I wondered. But I imagined you'd tell me in your good time, policeman's time.'

'I found an envelope in one of those secret drawers in your aunt's bureau. Someone had been there before me, but they hadn't taken all the evidence.'

He told her about the note and the impression of a heavy object that might have been in the envelope. She listened with interest and, he could have sworn, genuine surprise.

'It's a mystery to me. Honestly, Mr Brand. Of course I knew about the hidden drawer. Those old bureaux always have them. But my aunt never spoke to me about what was in it.'

'Have you any idea who the note could have come from?'

She shook her head. 'I haven't the least notion.'

'Could it be possible that there was another matching gold chain, like the one your aunt always wore, in existence?'

'There may have been, but I never saw one.'

'And "E", the initial on the note. That means

nothing?'

'It could be anyone, couldn't it?'

That's precisely what Waller had said. Brand sighed. 'Well, if you can think of any explanation and why someone desperately needed to get hold of it, let me know—or, better yet, Inspector Waller.'

He was dismally conscious that he was getting nowhere. If Joanna Saint-Clair knew anything she was convincingly keeping it hidden from him.

'How many people would have known about the drawer in the bureau?'

'Just about anyone who visited the house, I suppose. Charlotte took pride in showing off her things.'

'But not everything.'

'Apparently not.'

'And who could have had a key to the front door? There was no evidence of forced entry.'

'There were about half a dozen. Charlotte had two. I had one. The couple from the village. Two extras hanging on a hook in the kitchen.'

So much for security, thought Brand.

'One other thing.' He knew he was grasping at straws. 'Can you think of anything in your aunt's past that bothered her? That she was secretive about? Maybe her relationship with Leila Starr, the actress who committed suicide, for instance.'

'That was years before I came to live with her,

the poor relation she took in.' The sudden self-pity didn't become her. 'Sorry. Silly. No, she was obviously upset about Leila Starr. But by the time I came on the scene, she'd accommodated the tragedy into the story of her life, just as she accommodated everything else. To suit herself.'

'How do you mean?'

'Don't believe everything you read in the papers about Charlotte, Mr Brand. Her life was one big play-acting role. I think years ago she'd stopped being a real person and become a character in a huge spectacular devoted exclusively to herself. It's called perpetuating the image, Mr Brand. Now we really should go.' As they left the flat together, Brand felt his journey might not have been entirely wasted.

When she turned the key in the ignition of the Mini it obstinately refused to start. 'Damn. Starter motor keeps kicking out.'

She got out, opened the bonnet and with the confident use of a spanner freed the starter shaft.

She accepted his expression of approval with a mild show of pride. 'Not just a pretty face,' she laughed, shifting the car into first gear and heading it briskly on to the main road. Her capacity to surprise him, he mused, was apparently boundless.

# CHAPTER FIFTEEN

In his long life as a working police detective Ralph Brand had attended many press receptions, usually in his official capacity, sometimes just as an observer, occasionally, in his younger days, as a free-loader.

But the turn-out in the boardroom of Regent TV for the cast and executives of *Wild Fortune* was like nothing he'd experienced before. Shambles was too orderly a word for it. The media, *en masse*, thought Brand, resembled tribal hordes engaged in jungle warfare, everyone intent on getting the impossible, the exclusive quote and the exclusive picture. For the first time since Charlotte Saint-Clair's murder, the jackals were getting free access to those who were closest to her and, generously lubricated with liquor, they were making the most of it.

Reporters jostled noisily with photographers for vantage-points around the prime targets, Sam Ackerman, Liz Briley, John Arthur, the star designate, Elaine Pelham, should the series be continued and the Chairman of Regent TV who had been dragooned into putting in an appearance and patently wished he hadn't.

In a corner an earnest commercial radio interviewer was quizzing a bemused Lester

Ruddy about Charlotte's state of mind when he directed her last episode of *Wild Fortune*. The ITN news crew were huffily packing their gear and loudly describing the occasion as a dead loss. BBC *Sixty Minutes* had grandly turned down the invitation, hinting darkly that they had their own sources.

A ferocious young man in a green velvet jacket and expensively patched and paint-splattered jeans grabbed Joanna Saint-Clair firmly by the elbow the moment she arrived. 'Payne—*the Globe*. Knew your aunt very well, Jo.' She looked both pained at the familiarity and dubious about the intimacy he claimed with Charlotte Saint-Clair who, after all, wasn't around to dispute it.

'Let's find somewhere quiet.' He hustled her away before she had a chance to protest. 'Bimbo,' he called over his shoulder to a husky photographer, his neck lassoed with Leicas. 'I've got her. Quick. Before the others.'

'God! How am I supposed to control this mob? We should have hired the Albert Hall!' Mack Tully surveyed the scene with the gloomy resignation of a man who had given up an unequal battle in the certain knowledge that he'd be blamed for it later. 'Keep it quiet, dignified, they said. Quiet! Dignified!'

He glumly watched a reporter stub a cigarette out in a tray of *canapés*, while waving an empty glass with the other hand at a passing waiter who was having trouble keeping up with the demand.

He caught Brand's sympathetic eye. 'Well, you needn't think you'll get anything just standing there,' he said touchily with no attempt at the chummy courtesy for which he was famous. 'I suppose you're from *The Times*.'

Accepting what he judged to be a kind of compliment, Brand admitted that he wasn't from *The Times*. Mr Ackerman had asked him to come. 'Ralph Brand.'

'Oh, the ex-policeman. He wanted to talk to you. Don't know when I can get him free. Hang around.' He waved his hands in the direction of Ackerman who was fending off the onslaught of a tiny, birdlike woman of uncertain age with severely cropped grey hair and a voluminous black coat. Ackerman acknowledged the gesture, spotted Brand and nodded, mouthing 'Two minutes.'

'Well, well, if it isn't! Still getting into deep water, Ralph?'

Brand turned, recognizing the voice and its huge, burly owner instantly. 'Josh Buller, as I live and breathe.'

'Only just, as I understand it. Got a thump on the head last night, I hear. But you always did have a hide as thick as a rhino.'

Brand chuckled. He and Superintendent Josh Buller had been trading insults for more years than either cared to remember.

'Come up in the world, Josh? Nice to have you helping out on the case,' he said, enjoying needling the friend who used to call him 'sir'.

'What a circus! Bloody idiots, holding a Press reception—now. Might have known how it would turn out. Heaven knows, we warned them.'

'I thought you'd have better things to do with your time, Josh.'

'I have.' Buller selected a green olive from a saucer on a side table, chewed it grimly and spat out the pip in the palm of his hand. He studied it intently for a moment as if it contained the seed of all knowledge, then flicked it back in the saucer. 'It seemed a good idea to see what the clowns were up to. But I can't think anyone will be passing on secrets they shouldn't in this farce. I'm off.'

'Any ideas?'

'About this?'

'The case, Josh.'

'Haven't been on it long enough. But we're making headway. Pity your Inspector Waller got side-tracked by that nutter Billy Richards when the trail was still hot.'

'Waller had his reasons. Good reasons—at the time.'

'You didn't think so, obviously.'

'Well you know me. Doubting Thomas.'

'Don't I just. Look after yourself, old chap. That's an order.' He patted Brand affectionately on his broad back. 'I'll leave this rumpus to the boys.' He was referring to the two plainclothes policemen who'd been planted in the crowd.

'Going so soon, Superintendent?' Ackerman had managed to break loose from the throng and elbow a passage through to Brand.

'Not soon enough for me. Show business!' Buller heaved an exaggerated sigh and manoeuvred his way to the door.

Ackerman grinned, then his lined face became serious. He gripped Brand's arm tightly. 'Glad you came. I need to talk to you. Something Joe Gannis told me,' he said absently, not registering that the name meant nothing to Brand. 'It may be nothing, in which case forget it. But, well, see what you think.'

'Sam Ackerman, you can't get away from me that easily.' A rasping American monotone cut insistently into Ackerman's whispered conversation with Brand.

The beaky little woman in the black coat was plucking his sleeve. She even sounded like a crow, thought Brand.

'Meet me in my office, upstairs. You know where it is. We can talk privately. In about half an hour,' Ackerman murmured hurriedly into Brand's ear, then turned to the diminutive crow with a dazzling forced smile.

'Gloria! Sweetheart! What makes you think I want to get away from you?' He put his arm around her, hugging her to his chest. Having firmly insinuated herself back to the centre of his attention, she semeed grudgingly placated.

'Naughty Sam! You promised me an exclusive with the niece. But she cut me dead, the bitch. Something about *sub judice.*'

'Well, this is England, Gloria. A murder has been committed and there are laws about speaking out of turn while the police are conducting their investigations.'

'Don't give me that, Sam. Think of the publicity. Twenty million Americans read my syndicated column. It's not as if I want her to finger the killer, I just want her to tell me all she knows, to...'

'Finger the killer! Gloria, you're incorrigible. I'll see what I can do.'

'You'd better, Sam. You'd better.' There was an unmistakable threat in the woman's harshly monotonous voice. She was obviously adept at using goodwill as a weapon when it suited her.

'It's been a difficult time for her,' Brand volunteered, surprising himself by rushing in to Joanna Saint-Clair's defence.

The woman briefly switched her attention from Ackerman to Brand. He felt himself being sized up efficiently for his possible worth and status.

Ackerman gratefully seized on the diversion. 'Gloria, you really should meet Ralph Brand. He's a former police inspector who...' he chose his words carefully: 'He's helping on the case.'

The eyes in the birdlike face lit up, beady with interest.

'Gloria Beesley—Ralph Brand. I don't need to tell you, Brand, that Gloria is the most celebrated of all American show business columnists.' Ackerman was laying on the flattering so thickly it was laughable to all but Gloria Beesley, who accepted it as nothing but her due.

'My pleasure, Miss Beesley.' Brand grasped her extended claw.

'Have you turned up anything?' she waded in abruptly.

Brand ignored the question. He didn't intend to have his speculations about Charlotte Saint-Clair's murder trumpeted to twenty million avid American readers. 'Actually, Miss Beesley, Sam suggested I have a chat with you. I gather you knew Charlotte Saint-Clair from way back.' He found himself falling into the lingo of the lady. It was catching.

'No one knew her better. I can say that with absolute sincerity.' The flat vowels mangled the statement out of any meaning. Brand felt he wouldn't fancy being on the sharp end of any investigation conducted by Gloria Beesley.

'Perhaps we could meet. Tomorrow.'

'Sure. I'm at the Dorchester. Give me a call, any time. But I won't be around long. No story. They haven't even got a suspect yet. In the

States they'd have rounded up everyone who'd given her so much as the time of day in the weeks before her death by now.'

'Well, we do things differently here, Miss Beesley.'

'You sure as hell do.'

During the exchange of what Brand took to be pleasantries, Ackerman had disappeared. 'Well, I guess I'll give this Mack Sennett farce the elbow,' she croaked. Without another glance at him, she swept her cloak around her, accepted an anxious peck on the cheek from Mack Tully and, spotting more congenial company, bore down ruthlessly on the mild-mannered Chairman of Regent TV who viewed her approach with an expression of blank terror. Brand felt himself well and truly dismissed.

'What a creep!' Joanna Saint-Clair had sidled up to Brand with John Arthur in tow, taking good care to keep out of ear-and-eyeshot of Gloria Beesley. 'Can you imagine the first question she asked me? Who killed your aunt? Even if I knew, would I tell her?'

'She's just doing her job. That's how you get to be a syndicated columnist.' John Arthur's reasonable voice took the wind out of Joanna's anger. 'Jo's told me about you, Mr Brand. And Sam.'

In the midst of the frenzy, he carried a welcome air of sanity around with him, Brand observed. It was a knack some people had,

159

creating at least the appearance of order out of chaos.

'You haven't a drink. Can I get you one?'

Brand shook his head. 'I'll pass for the moment.'

'Wise decision. The good stuff's run out. They're on to the cheap plonk now. At least we can sit down now that it's thinning out. Jo tells me you got a nasty whack on the head last night.' His clipped accent, not quite English and not quite American, puzzled Brand briefly until he recalled that most show business people seemed to assume accents that probably didn't belong to them. Anyway John Arthur's concern appeared real enough.

Brand chuckled. 'I'd prefer not to be reminded. All the time I don't think about it it doesn't hurt.'

Casting his eyes at Joanna who was talking intently to Elaine Pelham, John Arthur drew Brand aside. 'I want to thank you for reading the riot act to Jo—about Russ Gilchrist. I've warned her about him before. But she can't see it. Underneath all that brisk exterior, she's a good-natured woman. I've a great respect for her and I wouldn't like to see her come to any harm.'

'She didn't seem inclined to pay any attention to *my* warning either.'

'Oh yes she did. You hit home. For some reason she trusts you and I'm glad. Anyway,

160

with a little luck and a lot of persuasion perhaps we can get her to go to the police. He's not safe on the loose.'

'Anything you can do to make her see sense.'

'You can count on me. Why are you shaking your head?'

'I'm wondering how anyone as calm and lucid as you has managed to survive in this crazy business.'

John Arthur scratched his head almost as if he wondered himself.

'It's not always this mad. Writing a great and famous TV series like *Wild Fortune* takes a lot of hard work, a little intuition and, above all, a monumental sense of humour.'

'I can imagine.'

'I doubt it, but thanks for the vote of confidence.'

They became aware that the conversation between Elaine Pelham and Joanna Saint-Clair behind them was becoming heated.

'Don't be a fool, Elaine,' Joanna was saying, then, realizing she could be overheard, bent closer to her companion and her words were lost in the general hubbub.

John Arthur caught Brand's alert reaction to Joanna's unguarded comment.

'Elaine—Elaine Pelham—have you met her? She wants to leave the series. Won't say why. She hasn't told Ackerman or the others and Jo's trying to talk her out of it. She'd be mad, of course. If and when it comes back she'd take over where Charlotte left off. We'd reshape it round her. It could make her name.'

'Maybe she just doesn't want to have her name made.'

'Have you ever met an actor or an actress who didn't want to be a star, even when they didn't admit it?'

Brand had the uncomfortable impression that he was being fobbed off with a plausible excuse for Joanna's remark. It could be the truth, a half-truth or a lie. In this strange frenetic atmosphere the divisions between the three were barely detectable, part of a large fantasy that the show business fraternity had created to accommodate the grim reality of why they were all there.

He remembered his promise to see Ackerman in his office. He looked forward to the peace and quiet and the amiable company of Ackerman relieved of the necessity to cosset the ego of Gloria Beesley and her like. More important, he was anxious to hear what Ackerman had to tell him.

Isolated in his own moody assessment of the alien situation in which he found himself, he excused himself after ten minutes or so to no-one in particular and took the lift up two floors to the producer's office. He paused in the empty corridor for a moment, relishing the silence and aware that he'd been standing for more than an hour in a hot, crowded room battered by strident chat on all sides.

He felt, quite suddenly, a despairing sense of loneliness, not for himself, but for Charlotte Saint-Clair whose memory had been reduced to the frantic pursuit of an item to fill tomorrow's newspaper or an interview to take up a few minutes of air time. Maybe it wouldn't have appalled her as much as it appalled him. Maybe this *was* Charlotte Saint-Clair's life or, at least, the necessary periphery of it.

He shrugged off the gloomy thought and ambled down the corridor. The secretaries had gone home, the doors of their cubicles shut. The outer office that led to Ackerman's was open. Brand tapped on the door, calling Ackerman's name. When there was no reply, he decided that the producer was probably still downstairs, waylaid by some other demanding reporter, which was more than likely.

But as he turned to go back, he heard a faint groan from the inner office. He pushed open the door wider.

Ackerman had indeed been waylaid. His all but lifeless body was slumped over his desk, the blotter oozing with the blood that seeped from a bullet wound in his chest. The brilliant light from a desk lamp gave the scene a hard, poster-like clarity. Ackerman lifted his powerful head, stared briefly, pleadingly, at Brand through shocked eyes and opened his mouth. But whatever he wanted to say Brand would never hear. As a trickle of blood traced from his mouth down his chin, he fell heavily forward, emitting a last, soft, dying breath.

In the presence of the still, dead body Brand experienced a spasm of guilt. 'Poor blighter! I should have thought,' he muttered, before summoning the help that was too late to save Sam Ackerman.

## CHAPTER SIXTEEN

By the time Ralph Brand wearily unlocked the door of the pokey, functional, single room he'd managed to book at short notice at the Grosvenor Hotel, the first sounds of early morning life were beginning to penetrate his window overlooking the concourse at Victoria Station. He found the muffled noises oddly comforting, blessedly normal after the abnormal events of the long night.

He'd given up all hope of sleep, his mind buzzing like a caged wasp with remembered sights, snatches of fractured conversations and, above all, the hubbub when the news had leaked through to the press on the premises of Regent TV that, while they'd been jockeying for gossip at a routine reception, Sam Ackerman was being murdered in the cloistered quiet of his office two floors above them.

With hard-nosed efficiency Josh Buller and his team of detectives and forensic experts had set in motion the machinery of gathering evidence. Brand didn't envy Buller his job and he hadn't enjoyed the comradely but searching interrogation to which he, Brand, had been submitted. He'd conducted many such inquisitions himself, but he'd never before been on the receiving end. It was an unnerving experience. Surprisingly, he found himself thinking like a criminal, monitoring his reactions, his answers, his gestures, fearing they might betray—what? With nothing to conceal, he nevertheless felt the sweaty burden of needing to prove an innocence which wasn't in question. It was an alarming reversal of roles for him and he wondered how many witnesses had squirmed as he had under the interrogations he'd conducted over his years on the Force. Witnesses whose only crime was that they'd been around when somebody else's crime had been committed.

All the time Buller had been grilling him politely, he'd been aware of the Superintendent's keen, probing eyes, alert, suspicious mind weighing the facts and finding them wanting.

'Just once more, Ralph. Take your time,' Buller had said patiently as if he were addressing a nervous child rather than a former detective who knew the game better than he did. 'Ackerman had asked you to meet him in his office. Now think, again, did he give any indication why he wanted to see you?'

'I've told you, Josh. None. I assumed, well, I suppose I must have known, it was something to do with Charlotte Saint-Clair's past.'

'Death?' Buller urged him.

'Don't put words into my mouth. There was no mention of her death. He said it might be nothing of importance. That's all.'

'Ralph, why didn't it occur to you to let us know?' Buller was choosing his words carefully so as not to offend his old superior, but the implication was plain. Brand had been negligent.

'It was no secret. Waller gave me Ackerman's message last night.' God forgive me, thought Brand. Was it always like this, searching for excuses, anything to shift the spotlight from oneself to someone else?

Then his old sense of authority and fairness re-asserted itself. 'No, I should have mentioned it. You're right.'

Buller relaxed as if Brand's admission were a small victory. They both understood the unspoken conclusion. If he had taken the police into his confidence maybe Ackerman wouldn't now be lying on a stretcher with dead eyes and a bullet through his heart.

'OK, Ralph. That's about it for now.' The

change in Buller's tone was marked. Having wrung the admission out of Brand, he was now treating him as an ally, a brother in arms. 'I suppose every crank in London will come forward to confess to the crime. Mind you, practically every crank *could* have done it. Half Fleet Street downstairs making such a racket no one could have heard a shot being fired up here. And in that crowd no one can be sure where anyone else was at a given time unless they were actually talking to them. You say you were alone when you decided to leave the party and come upstairs, Ralph?'

'As alone as you can be with a couple of hundred people around. By that I mean, the ones I had been talking to had drifted away.'

'Drifted out, most of them—the *Wild Fortune* lot anyway. The niece had gone, the cast, that director chap and the Chairman. Only—what's his name?—publicity, Tully, was left and the hard core of Fleet Street soaks.'

'Any trace of the weapon?'

Buller laughed sourly. 'You have to be joking! Anyone could have smuggled it out. But we're searching the place and we're taking statements from everyone. Not that we expect to turn up much here. Anyway, I'm grateful for the stuff on Gilchrist. Pity you couldn't get a better look at the gun he had. But I've put out an alert on him. Shouldn't be too hard to trace.'

'Unless he's gone into hiding.'

'In which case we've probably got our killer, haven't we.' It was a statement of confident fact, not a question. Brand couldn't argue the logic of it. A man goes into hiding because he has something to hide. Then he recalled how he'd felt, being questioned by Buller, when he hadn't anything to hide. It was all in the mind, manufactured guilts manufacture guilty responses.

As Buller was called away on more urgent matters, he put a fatherly hand on Brand's shoulder. And I could give him fifteen years, thought Brand, smarting under the paternalistic gesture. 'In future, Ralph, keep us informed. For everybody's sake, including your own. I'll be in touch.'

The words 'for everybody's sake' dinned into Brand's brain as he lay in the narrow bed, registering the gathering momentum of busy life in the railway terminal beneath his window. Something was missing, eluding him, just out of grasp of the tentacles of memory. He tried to block out his thoughts with a pillow, then gave up the struggle, took a shower, shaved, attacked the continental breakfast that had been left overnight in his room and discovered, to his surprise, that he felt refreshed and eager for action. The bump on his head was receding along with the ache.

The encounter with Buller had rankled, wounding his pride. He wasn't ready to be discarded on the scrap heap of senior citizens.

At a respectable hour, he telephoned the Dorchester and made an appointment with Gloria Beesley for that morning. He'd expected to have difficulty reminding her of his identity, but she'd instantly placed him. 'Make it eleven,' she'd croaked in that unmistakable rasping voice with its raw Southern California accent. 'We can share the hair of the dog.' She sounded as if she'd swallowed the dog the night before, he thought, recalling a memorable line from an old favourite movie of his, *All the King's Men*.

He whiled away an hour at Smith's bookstall on the station, reading the headlines of all the papers, most of which claimed that their correspondent had been on the spot when the second mysterious murder of a member of the *Wild Fortune* team had been committed. Their imaginative stories of being the last person to see Sam Ackerman alive—'his haunted, fear-ridden eyes will live in my mind forever' mourned the *Globe*—occupied Brand's time agreeably until he joined the queue for taxis, groaned when he noticed the one he'd chosen discouraged smoking and sympathized with the cabbie who complained that the traffic in Park Lane was 'something fierce'.

Almost before he knocked on the door of her suite at the Dorchester, Gloria Beesley opened it as if by telepathy. He decided, quite seriously, that she probably had a sixth sense. Anyone who

169

looked as much like a witch had to be one. As on the night before, she was dressed entirely in black: a black shift, cinched in at the waist with a black snakeskin belt, covering black leotards. Her cropped grey hair looked as if it had been freshly washed.

The room into which she led him was a chaotic confusion of half unpacked suitcases, crumpled newspapers strewn over the floor and the remains of breakfast, cups, plates, coffee-pot, scattered over every available side table. 'Welcome to the star witness,' she said gaily, 'the corpse-finder!'

Now Brand realized why she'd been so forthcoming. As the first on the scene of the crime, he was just grist to the mill of her column.

He was in two minds whether to play her along or smartly dispose of any misconceptions she had about his willingness to reveal all he knew to twenty million American readers when she instantly resolved the problem.

'Don't worry, I know enough about your antiquated laws in this country not to put you on the spot. I might just lean on you a little,' she said almost coquettishly. He realized she was much older than she had first appeared. Well into her seventies, but bearing up under the weight of years with a flamboyant refusal to acknowledge them as only American women seemed able to do.

'Then you won't mind if I lean back a little,' he responded in like manner.

Her deep chuckle developed into a throaty cough. 'Time for a bloody Mary,' she decided when she'd recovered. 'How about you?'

Brand was about to demur that it was a little early in the day for him, then realized that the implied criticism of her drinking timetable wouldn't go down too well with this formidable lady. 'A small one.'

'Now,' she said, settling herself in an easy chair and throwing her spindly leotarded legs over the arm defiantly. 'What can I do for you?' Before he could reply she was rattling on: 'Poor Sam! Nice guy, but soft. You have to be tough in this business. Maybe that's why he was killed. Conscience can make softies of us all.' Brand doubted whether she'd ever been guilty of softness in her life.

'Perhaps you can help. Solve his murder,' Brand said, not quite sure where the thought was leading, but deciding it was worth a try.

'Me?'

'Well, it's obviously tied in with Charlotte Saint-Clair's death.'

'You think so?' she said keenly.

'It's a fairly well founded guess, I'd say.'

She nodded. 'That's Charlotte for you. A walking disaster area. The beauty of it is, she never even knew it. Or if she did, she always managed to rationalize it.'

171

'Tell me about Charlotte Saint-Clair.'

She cupped her bloody Mary as if it were some sort of lifeline and gave another of those raucous laughs that had no humour in them. 'What was she really like? That's what they all ask. The trouble is, there's no true answer. When you're a star as big as Charlotte somewhere along the line the person becomes the image. It happened with Joan Crawford the same way. When I first met Charlotte in the 'thirties she was fresh from England, a bright-eyed, stunningly beautiful girl, still wet behind the ears, but oh so anxious to learn. I don't think I ever knew anyone with such driving ambition. You couldn't be that ambitious without making enemies. But the funny thing was no one seemed to nurse a grudge against her. She always came up smelling of roses!

'I was pretty green myself. I'd landed this job as Hollywood correspondent—well, that was the nice way of putting it. There was Louella and Hedda and Sheilah Graham and me. Those all-powerful gossip columnists you read about who could make or break careers,' she said derisively. 'Charlotte caught on quickly. She'd got this MGM contract. They were building her up big and she made it her business to play ball with publicity. She was a natural.'

'What about her relationship with Leila Starr?' Brand interrupted.

'That was the only out of character thing

about her,' Gloria remembered as vividly as if it happened only yesterday. 'Leila was the bad girl at the studio. Not really bad, but awkward. She didn't play the game according to the Hollywood rules. There were always scandals to be hushed up, live-in love-affairs at a time when no stars were supposed to sleep with anyone except their husbands or wives. Charlotte was always cast as the queenly heroine, Leila was the dizzy dumb blonde. Except she was neither dizzy nor dumb—nor blonde come to that. All that was a studio invention. Even her name. Her real name was Jackson. A poor girl from Boston—the wrong side of the tracks. The publicity department dreamt up the name "Starr" when she made a hit in her first bit-part as a wise-cracking cigarette girl in some B movie.'

'So what was the attraction between her and Charlotte?' said Brand.

'I thought at first it was the attraction of opposites. But then I realized it was stronger, deeper than that. They genuinely liked each other. It was the only time Charlotte had a set-to with Louis Mayer, the head of the studio. He warned her not to get too friendly with Leila. Not good for her image. But she paid no attention. She really stood up for Leila in the front office. That intrigued me. I'd always figured Charlotte was too ambitious to risk sullying that carefully groomed image. There was talk around Hollywood that they might have been having a Lesbian thing going for them. I never believed that. I saw too much of them. You know what I think?'

Brand shook his head.

'Fun! They had fun together. They could let their hair down and be themselves with each other. It was so simple none of those complicated Hollywood people caught on. They created drama on screen and they preferred to manufacture drama off screen as well.'

'What do you know about the gold chain Charlotte always wore?' said Brand.

'The one with which she was strangled? You're a policeman—or you were—what's your theory?' she asked him, making him work for the information she was giving him.

'I think there were two chains. Both with clasps made up of their initials.'

'Bullseye,' she chuckled. 'They were making a movie together. Charlotte the suffering heroine and Leila the bitch—as usual. They were doing a couple of days shooting in a little town just outside Hollywood and they found the two chains in some junk store. These days they'd call it an antique shop and charge the earth. But then it was just a junk store. I was visiting the movie lot doing a piece on the production. They were in high spirits. They seldom got to work together and they were having—like I said, fun. For some reason, they fell in love with those silly chains, bought them for a few dollars and when they got back to Hollywood they had those clasps specially made.'

'Charlotte kept one, Leila the other,' said Brand, stating the obvious.

'Right. It was a nothing thing to do, but it seemed to mean a lot to them. It was right after that that Leila really landed herself in trouble. She had an affair with a stunt man named Artie Nolan. Big, beefy guy, nothing upstairs but a dish to look at. He was killed doing some crazy stunt in a Western. Leila was damn near shattered by the tragedy. She really loved that dopey guy. At least for the time being. But the big trouble was that she was pregnant. The studio wanted her to get an abortion, but she refused. She had the baby, a boy. Again, the studio managed to hush it up and they persuaded her to let her sister in Boston bring up the boy.'

'E.' Brand recalled the initial on the note he'd found in Charlotte's cottage.

'E, what?'

'The sister. Ethel, Ella . . . ?'

'Emily. How did you know?'

'An educated guess.'

'I suppose I'm not allowed to ask where that education came from?'

'I'd rather you didn't.'

She shrugged. 'If you say so. But it goes

175

against the grain.'

'What happened between Charlotte and Leila after that?'

'I've never been able to find out,' she mused. 'But the relationship went sour. Not immediately. Not for a couple of years, but there was a cooling off. Charlotte had married a no-account actor—Chris Devane—and divorced him in a hurry. By then Leila had got over her grief for Artie. She was playing around again. It was about the beginning of the war. Neither of them were quite such big box office as they used to be. Things were changing in Hollywood. The studio were getting ready to dump Leila. She'd always been a nuisance. But all the time she was making money for them they put up with her little ways. When she stopped bringing in the big bucks she was expendable.'

'Was that the only reason why they wanted to get rid of her?'

'Not entirely. She'd become an embarrassment. As I said, she was no dumb blonde. She'd always been pretty outspoken in her views. Now she started speaking out of turn in support of left-wing causes.'

'Surely that was no crime then? Roosevelt in the White House, the New Deal.'

'Not strictly speaking. But studios didn't like their stars to be political. It gave the radical impression that they had minds of their own. Anyway Leila and MGM parted company—by mutual agreement, the statement said. No one believed it, of course. Leila took off on her own. To all intents and purposes, it was the end of Leila Starr so far as Hollywood was concerned.'

'But I remember she went on making pictures long after that.'

'You're quite a fan!' she said approvingly. 'Sure. It was one of those lucky chances that happened in Hollywood. Swings and roundabouts. Like Joan Crawford winning an Oscar for *Mildred Pierce* and Bette Davis making a comeback with *Whatever Happened to Baby Jane?* One of the poverty row studios took a chance on her in one of their classier movies. A new, mature image. Picture took off with the public. And, bingo, Leila was back in business.'

'But there was no reconciliation with Charlotte?'

'If there were it wasn't obvious. I was sorry. I liked those two. You should have seen them when they were together. Like two sides of a beautiful coin. One complemented the other. There's a still from that movie they did together. They used it on all the posters.'

Brand nodded, remembering.

'Joe Gannis did a lovely job on that picture,' she said.

The name which had sprung out of nowhere clicked into Brand's brain like a missing link that had been bothering him all through the last restless night. It was the name Sam Ackerman had mentioned in passing when he'd asked Brand to meet him in his office in the fateful hour before he met his death.

## CHAPTER SEVENTEEN

'Who is Joe Gannis?' Brand tried to make it sound casual, a disinterested comment thrown idly into the conversation. But he had the feeling that he wasn't fooling Gloria Beesley. The beady eyes, framed in boot black mascara and eyeliner, seemed to penetrate into his mind, willing him to elaborate.

'Sam Ackerman said he'd seen him on the day he died—yesterday,' Brand volunteered.

'Good Lord! Is he still alive? He must be older than I am. I haven't heard of him in years. Joe was one of the best lighting cameramen in Hollywood. The old Hollywood.' She caught Brand's question before he could ask it. 'Director of photography on a movie. He lit all of Charlotte's big films. When she was in a position to make demands, she always insisted on Joe. Most of the major stars had their favourite. William Daniels was Garbo's. Joe was Charlotte's.'

'How close would a lighting cameraman be to a star?'

'Probably closer than anyone, short of her

mother or her current husband. It doesn't matter how many affairs she has, he is—or was—her constant lover. The one who cements her relationship with that great god out there— the public. A good lighting cameraman can make a star look like a million dollars on the screen, or a has-been.'

'I gather when you talk about a constant lover, you don't mean it's a physical relationship,' he said with a delicacy she seemed to find amusing.

'Heavens, no. Well, hardly ever. It's much more spiritual and, at the same time, more practical than that.'

'I suppose then he'd know a lot more about the star personally than most people.'

'Sometimes. It depends.'

'Did Joe Gannis know Charlotte Saint-Clair well?'

'You take a roundabout way, but you get there in the end, don't you, Mr. Brand?' she laughed. 'What you're really trying to ask me without actually saying it is: why would Ackerman take the trouble to look up Joe Gannis yesterday?'

Brand nodded. 'Something like that.'

'Frankly, I wouldn't have the faintest idea, but I can make the same guess you're making. For ten, fifteen years, all the time she was at the top in Hollywood Joe was probably privy to just about every secret Charlotte might have had.

When you lead as public a life as she did you have to have someone you can trust to confide in. So far as Charlotte was concerned, Joe was it.'

'What happened to him?'

'He retired sometime in the middle nineteen-fifties. He must have been nearly sixty at the time. As long as I can remember him he never seemed young. He'd come to Hollywood from England when they were importing talent from all over the world. Prided himself on keeping his British nationality. I guess that's why he and Charlotte hit it off. They had some great years, great pictures together. He left Hollywood about the same time that Charlotte did. I suppose he settled in England. He must have made a decent pile while he was there.'

'Why did Charlotte leave?' He was enough of a movie addict to know the answer but he wanted Gloria Beesley's version of it.

'The natural order of things. She was getting older, the audiences were getting younger. She had the sense to see the writing on the wall. So she quit while she was still fairly near the top and, as you know, she was sufficient of a name to come back here and continue her career, instead of wilting away by her swimming pool waiting for her agent to phone. I admire her pluck. She always said, "I'm not yet ready to play Marilyn Monroe's mother". Well, she outlived Marilyn, didn't she?'

'And Leila Starr?'

'Catastrophic! She was one of Hollywood's tragedies. After her comeback she was riding high. But it was the time of the Communist witch-hunt in Hollywood after the war. Anyone who'd ever signed their name to a left-wing cause or donated a dollar to Russian aid was at risk. Leila was called before the UnAmerican Activities Committee. She was one of their test cases. She took the Fifth Amendment, refused to name names. I don't think she even knew any names or had anything to hide. She was just a natural-born liberal.'

'Why particularly was she singled out?'

'Why not? It was the way things were then. Anyway it was the end of her career. She was black-listed. Producers were scared to hire her. Bad for box office. It happened to a lot of people then. Some were survivors. They came back. Leila didn't. She virtually disappeared. Occasionally, you'd see her name in *Variety*, appearing in summer stock or off Broadway. But then nothing. The next thing I heard was that she'd committed suicide. It didn't even make the headlines. Just a few paragraphs in the centre pages. She'd been away too long. People had forgotten.'

'And no one ever discovered what had happened to her son?'

'I guess no one bothered to find out. Leila was yesterday's news long before she swallowed a quart of whisky and an overdose.'

Brand remained silent for a minute or two. Gloria Beesley's matter-of-fact recital of a story that was just 'yesterday's news' had moved him more than he cared to reveal. For some reason he couldn't quite fathom, Leila Starr's tragedy had cast Charlotte in a new, different light. But there was something more he needed to know. Something that perhaps Sam Ackerman had found out on the day he was killed. And the one person who could supply the answer was an old man named Joe Gannis who must now be well over eighty.

Gloria Beesley waved her hand across his face. He noticed that her be-ringed fingers were arched with arthritis.

'Still with me?' she rasped. 'There's nothing like old Hollywood stories for sending people to sleep. I've got a million of them.'

'This one's enough,' said Brand, jerking himself out of his mournful musing on the fate of Leila Starr. 'I'm very grateful to you, Miss Beesley.'

'Let's say you owe me one, Mr Brand. When you catch the killer I want to be the first to know.'

'What makes you think I'm out to catch a killer?'

'I think I know you, Mr Brand. You're a strange one. A real lone ranger, I'd guess. They could put you in a movie. Only it's a pity John

Wayne isn't alive to play you. All those dead, wonderful people!' she said with a strange softness, as if in remembering the mortality of others she was anticipating her own.

★　　　★　　　★

Sam Ackerman's secretary was in the middle of clearing out her dead employer's desk when Brand phoned. He knew because she told him so at great length between fits of weeping. No one, it seemed, could have been a nicer boss, even though he could be a little sharp at times, but that was only when he had things on his mind. But he always remembered Christmas and birthdays and days off for shopping.

No, she couldn't recall anything about a man named Mr. Gannis, but then everything was in such chaos at the office, with all those policemen nosing around, asking what she considered improper questions. As if anyone would *want* to murder Mr Ackerman. She felt very strongly that it was a slur on his character even to suggest such a thing. Well, yes, someone had shot him. But it had to be some kind of maniac. Surely?

Patiently Brand listened to the distraught woman, making sympathetic noises when it seemed appropriate. Then when she appeared to be running out of steam, he explained quietly and firmly who he was, who Joe Gannis was and when Sam Ackerman might have got in touch with him.

There was a long pause at the other end of the telephone, so long that Brand wondered whether he'd been cut off. But, finally, she came back. 'Sorry', she apologized, 'just one of those awful policemen wanting to know where Mr Ackerman—' she choked on the name, then recovered her composure quickly—'Mr Ackerman kept his confidential files. I told him Mr Ackerman kept his *confidential* files in his head. Everyone had access to the rest of them in the office here.

'Yes, I do remember now you had an appointment with Mr Ackerman. And that Mr Gannis, now that you mention him, I can't think how I forgot. He caused me a great deal of trouble.' She sounded aggrieved, as secretaries do when their routine has been disrupted. 'He must have slipped my mind, what with the shock and everything.'

Brand politely steered her away from the shock and everything. He had an uncomfortable feeling that time was pressing. His time. He couldn't explain it. It was just that old nervous, unaccountable sensation that something crucial was about to happen. Soon.

'What was the problem with Mr Gannis?' he prodded.

'Finding him,' she said abruptly, as if he should have known without her telling him. 'It was on the morning of that dreadful reception.'

Another long pause.

'And . . .?'

'In the middle of all the arrangements. It was short notice for the Press, you see, and the phones never stopped ringing. In the middle of all that, he told me to locate this man, Joseph Gannis. He'd been something in the film industry in Hollywood. He wasn't even sure if he were still alive. Well, I looked in the telephone directory first.'

Now that she was in full flood, Brand sensed it would be a long story but with a little judicious prompting he might cut it short.

'The telephone directory didn't help,' he volunteered.

'No. So then I phoned the ACTT—The Association of Cinema and Television Technicians. They knew of him, but his membership had lapsed years ago.'

Oh Lord, Brand cursed silently. All he wanted was the man's address, not his history. 'But you did find him, in the end?'

'Well, yes. Quite by chance. I got his address from the British Film Institute. Apparently they knew him quite well. Very reverent they were about him. I suppose they would be. Famous in Hollywood, they said. Not that I'd ever heard of him.'

After what seemed like eternity, Brand elicited the information she could have given him in ten seconds. Joe Gannis lived in Lupus

185

Street in Pimlico.

'What's his telephone number?'

'Oh, he doesn't have a telephone. Can you imagine, these days? Mr Ackerman had to go round and see him—on the off-chance. It was very inconvenient.'

'Then I suppose I'll have to go round and see him—on the off-chance,' Brand sighed. Everything in this case seemed to operate on the off-chance.

He thanked her profusely, expressed his sympathy yet again and suggested that she might be advised to give this information to the police.

But not, hoped Brand, before I've had a chance to see him. He didn't want one of Josh Buller's bright young men with their crisp questions and forbidding efficiency queering his pitch. At least Lupus Street wasn't a million miles away.


## CHAPTER EIGHTEEN

Urgency suggested a taxi. But Brand took a bus to Pimlico. He relished the opportunity to organize his thoughts while taking in the still pleasantly maintained atmosphere of London's 'stucco paradise' on the embankment of the Thames with its neat rows of tall, terraced houses to which butlers and ladies' maids used to retire from the grand residences of Mayfair and Belgravia where they'd been in service to the gentry.

Now most of those houses had been turned into modest hotels and colonies of apartments for London's shifting population. But the aura of a more gracious age remained in the quiet, green squares and the proportion of elderly residents who clung tenaciously to the illusion of days gone by as they pottered querulously in the small shops or took their ease under the trees in St George's Square.

Lupus Street, so named as a long-forgotten tribute to the son of the second Marquess of Westminster, dissected the area in a surgically straight line along which Brand tramped purposefully until he found the address Ackerman's secretary had given him. Like its neighbours, it had been converted into flats. A scrawled surname beside a bell indicated that Joe Gannis lived in the basement. As Brand rang the bell, a tabby cat meowed lazily, then addressed itself to a saucer of milk on the doorstep.

He waited patiently, undaunted by the fact that at first there was no reply. A recluse in his eighties, Brand reasoned, would be likely to take his time. Persistently, he rang again and was rewarded with a sound of shuffling feet and loud demands to keep his hair on from behind the door.

A small, shrunken man in a shapeless pullover and carpet slippers flung the door open wide. 'Not today,' he barked, not belligerently but as a matter of course. For all his sloppy clothing, he looked curiously dapper, his movements swift and decisive. A trim, white beard and piercing cornflower-blue eyes gave his leathered old face the appearance of an alert, ageing pixie.

'I'm not selling,' said Brand agreeably.

The old man scrutinized him carefully, nodding as he did so. 'You don't look the type,' he agreed. 'But I'm not voting for anyone either and I don't have opinions about detergent, ice-cream or conservation.' He spoke with the loud authority of the hard of hearing. There were traces of the faint American accent acquired by someone who had lived a long time in the States but hadn't totally succumbed to the colloquial twang.

Brand decided that, for all his great age, he wasn't a man to mess about with. He came straight to the point.

'I gather you're Mr Gannis,' he said, not bothering to wait for a reply. 'Sam Ackerman came to see you yesterday. You gave him some information that he wanted to tell me. But he didn't get the chance. By the way, my name's Ralph Brand.'

'Ackerman. Good lad!' The old man nodded

188

again. Brand supposed that to Joe Gannis, Ackerman *had* seemed just a 'lad', a supposition borne out by his next remark. 'Worked with me, donkey's years ago. Assistant camera operator. Bright, eager boy. Always knew he'd go far.'

He looked grudgingly at Brand. 'I guess you want to come in.'

'If I'm not interrupting anything.'

'What's to interrupt?' He stood aside and ushered Brand into the small hall which led into a large, roomy living-room, surprisingly light since part of its huge window looked out on to the basement area steps.

For a moment Brand stood on the threshold, adjusting his eyes to the amazing sprawl of the room. The walls were decorated with huge blown-up prints of film stills and exquisitely posed photographs of the great Hollywood stars now mostly dead or in their dotage. It was like wandering into the foyer of one of those great picture palaces of the 1930s with their regal names which fed the fantasies of the multitudes during the golden days of filmgoing.

Joe Gannis stood back enjoying Brand's incredulity. 'All my lovelies!' he gloated. 'Photographed them all in my time. How about a cuppa?' His mind darted agilely from one subject to the next as if age were imposing a time limit on his thoughts.

Brand followed him into the tiny kitchen and

189

looked around him approvingly. It was impeccably tidy, a place for everything and everything in its place. He recognized the same *trait* in himself. The neatness was the last resort of an orderly mind applying itself to the *minutiae* of life which was all that was left to it.

'Now, what's this about Ackerman?' said Joe Gannis cheerfully as he poured the tea from an enormous brown teapot and carefully measured in the milk.

For a moment Brand couldn't believe his ears.

'Don't you know?'

'Know what?'

'He's dead. Murdered. Yesterday. Soon after he saw you.'

The old man's frail body sagged heavily into a chair. 'So that's what it was all about!' He seemed to be musing to himself. Then he became aware of Brand and also that some sort of explanation was required.

'I wouldn't have known. Don't watch television or read newspapers. Hardly ever turn on the radio.'

He noticed Brand's disbelieving eyes turning to the twenty-six-inch screen television set in the corner. 'That's not for watching,' explained Joe Gannis. 'Beastly rubbish! That's for *them*.' He pointed to the shelves behind Brand's back which were stacked high with video cassettes of old movies. A video recorder sat on the floor beside them.

He shook his old head. 'Well, well, Sam, dead! Hadn't seen him for so long. Don't see many people at all. I was the one who told him to get out of Hollywood before the rot set in. Television!' He uttered the word as if a strong, unpleasant smell was attached to it. 'So he gets out and what does he end up doing? Television. Ah well, everyone dies, sooner or later. But I wonder who'd have wanted to kill Sam?'

'Maybe you know, Mr Gannis. Without knowing it, so to speak.' Brand explained his own interest in the case which Joe accepted without question. It was part of the shorthand he'd developed for living the rest of his left-over years. He'd obviously decided that Brand was all right and the formalities were extraneous and time-wasting.

'That makes two of them then. Charlie—well, I always felt it would catch up with her. But Sam!'

'You didn't like Charlotte Saint-Clair?' said Brand. 'I thought...'

Joe Gannis cut him short. 'I loved her. Oh, not in that sense. But we made magic on the screen. Most glorious face I've ever photographed. The camera adored her. But I couldn't forgive her for what she did.'

'You must have seen each other when you returned to England?'

'Nope. Never once. And never regretted it.

She knew. Oh, she knew, all right. She also knew I'd never talk—not while she was alive anyway.'

'Mr Gannis, can you tell me what you told Sam Ackerman? Can you recall?'

Joe Gannis looked aggrieved. 'Sure thing. Nothing wrong with my memory, even if the old carcass doesn't work as well as it used to. Who else have you spoken to?'

'Gloria Beesley.'

'That old hag!' Joe chuckled, which made him look even more like a mischievous pixie. 'Well, she knew Charlie pretty well, but not like I did.'

'Why did Sam Ackerman come to you in the first place? Yesterday.'

'He'd been nosing through some old cuttings on Charlotte and Leila. Something had set him thinking. I guess you must have been the one to spark it off. Anyway, he wanted to know all about the split between Charlie and Leila.'

'Would that be after Charlotte's marriage and divorce?'

'About then.' He wrinkled his brow. 'No, later. Had to be. The marriage slipped everybody's mind. Most of all Charlie's. It was when she and Leila were both fighting for their careers and I mean fighting. After the war. The youngsters were coming up, the public wanted new faces. It was almost like nineteen-thirty all over again when talking pictures came in.'

'But what had that got to do with the coldness between Charlotte and Leila?'

'Don't rush me, sonny.' Brand couldn't remember the last time he'd been addressed as 'sonny', perhaps by some forbidding sergeant when he'd been a novice copper. He let it pass with a quiet smile. Joe Gannis was clearly determined to tell his tale at his own pace.

'Most of Hollywood thought there was some hassle between them over a guy. I knew it was nothing like that. They'd often shared boyfriends. But that wasn't what drove them— sex. It was ambition. There was a huge best-seller at the time. *A Woman Condemned.* MGM had the film rights. It was supposed to be the biggest thing since *Gone With The Wind.* Both girls wanted that picture so badly. Wonderful part for an actress in it and there weren't too many of those around. They were mostly making tough guy pictures then, with big male stars. Peck, Lancaster, Douglas, Mitchum. Anyway, the casting for *A Woman Condemned* narrowed down to Charlie or Leila.'

'I remember it. Charlotte Saint-Clair made the movie. Didn't turn out very well, did it?' said Brand.

'Too right it didn't. That's the irony of it. She went to all that trouble and it didn't do a thing for her. Sort of poetic justice, I suppose.'

'How do you mean?'

'Well, right in the middle of the preproduction publicity over who would get the part, suddenly Leila was out of the running. The House UnAmerican Activities Committee started investigating her and her so-called Communist affiliations. There were headlines all over the place. She was summoned to testify, to name names—secret Party members infiltrating the Hollywood unions, that kind of garbage.'

'I heard about that.'

'Sure you did. Big star tagged a left-wing subversive. It was news. But dear, stubborn Leila, she wouldn't play ball with them. She was what they called an unfriendly witness. For the life of me I don't know why she did it. I don't think she had anything to hide or knew any names to name. She'd signed her name to left-wing causes, donated to Soviet charities during the war, but so had a lot of people at the time.

'Maybe it was just sheer, wonderful cussedness on her part—bravado!' Gannis mused. 'Maybe she saw it as the greatest role of her career—telling that Committee where they got off. She was splendid.'

He flicked his eyes at a large photograph of Leila Starr in her later years over his mantelpiece. The perky young blonde had matured over the years, but the same sardonic smile played around her lips, the eyes were just as challenging as they'd been when she'd tempted many a young hero to commit some

194

indiscretions. Yes, judged Brand, this was a woman who'd enjoy the risk of standing up and being counted, with no thought of the possible aftermath.

'At first I don't think she had any idea how her stand would kill her career stone dead,' Joe Gannis continued as if reading Brand's mind. 'The lefties applauded her. But after that no one in the Hollywood establishment—the producers, the movie tycoons who mattered—would give her the time of day. You have to remember what it was like during the Communist witch-hunts in America after the war, everyone was nervous of being black-listed. If a star was tainted, their pictures wouldn't get screen-time.'

'But what had all this to do with Charlotte?'

Joe Gannis stared keenly at Brand. 'You're a former policeman, so you said. Can't you guess?'

'Charlotte tipped off the Committee?'

'Not just tipped them off—everyone knew of Leila's liberal leanings. Charlie gave them chapter and verse, every last detail and a lot more invented ones. And as a reward, even though she wasn't an American citizen, they promised to keep her name right out of it. And they kept their promise. There was no hint that Charlotte had turned on her old friend.'

'Then how did you learn this?'

'It wasn't until quite a while after. I'd had

some suspicions. But nothing concrete. It was during the last picture we made together out there. Charlotte knew she was about finished in Hollywood. She was no longer box office. She was uncertain about her future and worried about how she'd be received back in England.'

The old man paused for a moment, relishing the suspense, as much for himself as for Brand. 'I took her out one night to cheer her up, I thought. A few laughs, a couple of drinks. But she got more drunk than I'd ever seen her. She never could hold her liquor. We got to talking about the old days and Leila. She became maudlin and it all spilled out. She was weeping into her booze. Can't stand a tearful drunk. But I listened. The next morning when she'd sobered up, she realized what she'd told me. We never spoke about it. But I guess ever after that she felt too uncomfortable around me and, frankly, I felt too uncomfortable around her.'

'Do you mean she'd actually dump her old friend in the soup like that—just for a part in a film?'

'Just for a part in a film!' Joe Gannis repeated mockingly. 'Mr Brand, never underestimate the ego and ambition of a certain kind of star. They'd kill their mothers and disown their children to protect that one, big, glorious thing in their lives—their star status.'

'Leila didn't.'

'Leila was different, so are a lot of other

196

people in this business. They aren't all Charlies. But to Charlie being a star was food, drink and the breath of life. Without it, she'd die.'

'Did Leila ever know who'd shopped her?'

'She never said. But I guess she did. But she had her pride. If she was down, she didn't whine. And maybe it was a small triumph for her—keeping quiet. Heaven knows, she needed some kind of triumph. In any case, when it was all over what was the point of pinning it on Charlie? And I don't think she had the heart to care any more after those hearings. She was through. Nothing could reverse that. She went back home to Boston, to her sister and her boy. I visited her a couple of times before I returned to England. It was like meeting a zombie. She was drinking heavily. Drugs, too, probably. Oh, she tried to make a comeback, but it didn't take. I knew she wouldn't last much longer. And I was right. Soon after, she committed suicide.'

'It must have been pretty traumatic for her sister and Leila's son.'

'You bet. Emily nursed a mighty hate for Charlie. But it was all inside her, festering. If she'd been alive when Charlie was strangled, I'd have thought she did it. But she, too, was long dead.'

'Do you know what happened to the boy?'

'He must have been in his teens when his mother died and then his aunt. Last I heard he left Boston. But I didn't keep track. It was all another time.'

'No clue at all?'

'No. But I'll tell you one thing, Mr Brand. Kids with show business parents often end up in show business themselves.'

Brand digested the remark thoughtfully. It coincided with the suspicion he'd been nursing over the past two days. The chances were that Sam Ackerman had arrived at much the same conclusion. And, with a faint shiver, Brand realized it had probably cost him his life.

'He'd be in his early forties now, wouldn't he? The son?'

'Give or take a little.'

Brand finished his cold tea and took leave of the old man, cautioning him that he should go to the police with his information.

Joe Gannis chuckled impishly. 'Never have any truck with the law, that's my motto. Present company excepted. But you seem a regular sort of fellow. I figure they can find me if they want to. After all, you did.'

Brand smiled. Joe Gannis was quite a character. As he let himself out of the front door, the tabby cat padded past him and wound itself round Joe's bandy leg. The old man bent down and gently smoothed his hand down its coat. The tabby purred.

'Cats are better than people. They don't ask questions and they know when to leave you alone,' he said as he shut himself away with his glossy photographs, his videos and his memories.


## CHAPTER NINETEEN

'Gossip, Ralph, gossip! The reminiscences of some elderly Hollywood reporter whose memories are probably no more reliable than the facts in her column! And the ramblings of an old boy in his dotage!'

John Waller had been listening to Brand with barely concealed impatience. Only a few minutes before he'd suffered a testy phone call from Superintendent Josh Buller who had been less than complimentary about the efforts of the Sussex constabulary. The relationship between the Metropolitan police and the provincial forces was at best uneasy. When the two were in collaboration the joint investigation could be an unnerving obstacle course, particularly for the junior partner, as Brand well remembered.

Waller paced the floor of his office restlessly, pausing now and then to study intently a spot on the cord carpet as if it might reveal some elusive clue he'd overlooked.

'Granted,' he agreed. 'Charlotte Saint-Clair was murdered by someone with a grudge against her.'

'Someone with a sense of humour—or, rather, a sense of the absurd.'

Waller looked in amazement first at his Sergeant, Bob Essex, perched uncomfortably on the arm of a chair, and then back at Brand. 'What the hell's *that* supposed to mean?'

'To kill someone as celebrated as she was with the gold chain that was almost her trademark! Wouldn't you say there was a sort of comic irony in that?'

Waller raised his hand wearily. 'Anything you say, Ralph. But it isn't relevant.'

'I'd say it was very relevant.'

Waller ignored the remark. 'And Ackerman was killed because somehow he'd stumbled on the identity of the murderer and, more important, the evidence to put him away. *Ergo*, let's stop chasing shadows, Ralph. Russ Gilchrist has done a bunk. He had the motive for killing Saint-Clair because he thought she'd ruined his career.'

Brand nodded. 'He was in the vicinity when the crime was committed. He had the weapon that was probably used on Ackerman. I know all that, John. But it still doesn't sit right.'

'Well, see how this sits. You haven't given me time to tell you what's been happening in this neck of the woods. Joanna Saint-Clair and Gilchrist were very close. Right? If anyone other than Ackerman could nail him, she could. Right? For your information, she narrowly escaped being killed herself today. Her car went out of control and careered into a tree. Fortunately, she was in low gear, just starting off, doing barely ten miles an hour. We examined the car. The brakes had been tampered with. If she'd been driving at speed she'd have been a goner.'

The unexpected news acted on Brand like a blow to the stomach. He'd warned her that she might be in some kind of danger from Gilchrist, but he hadn't anticipated anything so cold-blooded, so calculated.

'Where did it happen?'

'In the lane outside her aunt's cottage. We'd mopped up everything we'd needed to do there and she'd decided to return, clear up things, set the wheels in motion to sell it. Understandably.'

'Was she badly hurt?'

Waller shook his head. 'No. Just shaken up a bit. No damage. A few bruises. She's a plucky lady. Kept her head when she realized what was happening. Steered it deliberately into the tree.'

'Where is she now?'

'Back at the house. Wouldn't hear of going into hospital. And the couple who came in from the village said they'd stay with her as long as she wanted. I guess she's safe enough for the time being. Gilchrist wouldn't go near the place now. Ralph, it's just a matter of time. We'll get him. Every police station has an alert out for him—and the airports. His passport is missing, naturally. Just a matter of time,' he repeated.

'Then why are you behaving like a cat on a hot tin roof? Can't just be the bollocking from Buller. You've had worse than that from me in your time.'

Waller glanced at Essex. 'Think you could rustle up some coffee, Bob?' The Sergeant took the hint and excused himself gratefully from what threatened to develop into a private argument.

'Sorry, John. Shouldn't have said that in front of...'

'That's all right. Decent bloke. Discreet.'

'Not my prime virtue, I'm afraid. But you didn't answer my question, though.'

Waller sighed heavily. His respect for the older man, rooted in their years of working together, was unbounded. But sometimes he drove him to distraction. 'It's you, Ralph. You and your theories. Your bloody instinct. You can never take simple, incontrovertible facts at their face value. You always have to screw them up. And then you screw me up. Sometimes...'

'You just wish I'd retire gracefully like everyone else and leave you to do your job. You're absolutely right, John. I should. You, Buller, have all the evidence you need to wrap up the case, both cases. Forget what I said. I'll just potter along.'

'And make a nuisance of yourself and probably get clobbered again. No, Ralph, that won't do. You've started, so you'd better finish. You're not happy about the Gilchrist theory. Why? Come on, give me chapter and verse. Convince me.'

Brand, who had remained standing throughout their fraught conversation, plumped himself in the one easy chair in the office and took out his pipe, fingering it thoughtfully, but not attempting to fill or light it. 'As you say, it's just instinct. Nothing hard,' he said finally. 'But in my experience you have to fit the character of the man to the crimes he's supposed to have committed.'

'Come off it, Ralph. You know as well as I do that all murders which aren't committed by hardened villains or the mob are irrational. A solid, law-abiding citizen who's put up a respectable front for thirty years suddenly kills his wife. A woman under pressure driven out of her wits by a crying baby smothers it with a pillow. There's precious little logic about murder.'

'But don't you see, John, these murders weren't irrational, they weren't committed on the spur of the moment "under pressure"—though I grant you Ackerman's was probably a panic reaction. Whoever strangled Charlotte Saint-Clair must have been planning it for a long time. If they just wanted her dead they could have picked a dozen other more— more sensible ways, if you like. A handy accident, for instance. You know as well as I do that many such cases of murder are never solved because they're never proved to be murder in the first place.'

'Go on,' Waller replied. 'All you're doing is quoting the rule book at me.'

'In every respect, down to the manner in which she was killed, Charlotte's murder was a punishment that fitted *her* crime. It was planned for her to know as she died *why* she was being killed. It was revenge, John.'

'So? Gilchrist had cause for revenge, so he thought,' Waller argued.

'But Gilchrist wasn't, isn't, the kind of man capable of biding his time, fooling everyone, picking the right moment. He's a man of impulse. A sudden explosion of temper—that I grant you. But I'd lay odds from what I saw of him, he couldn't carry anything like this through.'

'Unless he had help,' said Waller carefully. 'have you thought about that?'

'It's crossed my mind.' It had, too, but he hadn't wanted to dwell on it, consider its obvious implications.

'Besides, Gilchrist's an actor. Not a good one, perhaps. But he's trained to play a part. It's not unknown for actors to confuse the fantasy of their profession with reality.'

Brand shook his head. 'I still can't buy Gilchrist.'

'Well, you can't deny he's behaving damned suspiciously if he's innocent. Anyway, Ralph, it's all hypothetical now. They'll bring him in sooner or later and I can't tell you what pleasure it'll give me to see you eat your words,' said Waller agreeably.

Brand sucked hard on his dead pipe. 'I'm talking but you're not listening.'

'You ought to light that thing.'

Brand ignored him. 'All right, let's shelve Gilchrist. Did Buller get a rundown on the people who'd worked with Charlotte Saint-Clair recently? How many of them have lived in the States?'

'The lot! Sometime or other. Mack Tully, Lester Ruddy, John Arthur, Ray Harding, Elaine Pelham—Ackerman of course. Not forgetting Gilchrist. Show business! It's a movable feast these days. They go where the work is. Europe, America.'

'And they're all in their early forties?'

'More or less.'

'What about Elaine Pelham? When I was at that reception I overheard an argument between her and Joanna Saint-Clair. The niece said, as I recall, "don't be a fool, Elaine".'

'You're really clutching at straws, Ralph. Have you seen the evening paper?'

Brand shook his head as Waller handed him the London tabloid. On the front page there was a becoming photograph of Elaine Pelham with a long caption in bold type. Brand read it carefully. 'Elaine Pelham made a statement through her agent this morning that she wouldn't be renewing her contract for another series of *Wild Fortune* if Regent TV should decide to continue with the show after the deaths of Charlotte Saint-Clair and its producer, Sam Ackerman. She refused to comment except to say, "It would be too macabre, too ghoulish." Her agent announced that she was considering an offer to join the Royal Shakespeare Company.'

'That satisfy you?' said Waller when Brand had finished.

Brand scrutinized the item again. He hated to admit it but it would certainly account for the heated discussion he'd witnessed the evening before. Elaine Pelham was well liked both by her colleagues and the public. If she left the show, if and when it returned, its popularity would undoubtedly plunge after the first flush of curiosity value which, in her own quoted words, would be simply macabre and ghoulish.

'What about the second chain and the note I found in Charlotte's home the other night?' He knew he was, as Waller had remarked, clutching at straws. He had no evidence to offer, only a nagging feeling that somewhere along the line the police were missing out.

As if reading his thoughts, Waller replied gently, 'We've only your word about another chain and you admit you didn't even see it, you just thought it might have been there. As to the note, where is it? Ralph, you did suffer a bump on the head that night.'

'Which doesn't mean I'm not right in the head. And what about that? I didn't thump myself, you know.'

'A sneak thief, a curious kid maybe, even a snooping reporter.'

'You can't seriously believe that?'

'I don't seriously believe *anything*, until someone presents me with the facts and evidence I can act on.' For all the affection he felt for his former Inspector, the exasperation in Waller's voice sounded dangerously close to breaking-point.

'I'll get you the facts, the godalmighty evidence.' It was a rash, stupid remark and Brand knew it.

'Oh no you won't, Ralph. I've had it. I've had you. Go home. Get some sleep. Leave it to us. I promise I'll let you know as soon as anything breaks. You've been a big help. You got that poor little bugger, Billy Richards, off the hook. I'm grateful. But you've done enough. You can't do any more.'

Brand sensed the anxiety behind his friend's angry tirade. There was nothing to be gained by pursuing the matter. He needed some quiet, alone with himself and his thoughts.

'Perhaps you're right,' he conceded.

His conciliatory tone didn't fool Waller.

'Promise?'

'I said, perhaps you're right. I'll sleep on it.'

'OK, old sport. I believe you. But I can't help remembering you're a devious bugger. Now, do me a favour, clear out and let me get on with my job. I just wish someone would tell *me* to sleep on it.'

'Give my regards to Buller.'

'I'd like to give him something, but it wouldn't be regards.' Waller chuckled.

He watched the big, bulky man, now slightly stooped, in his shapeless tweed jacket, plod down the corridor and out of the station. He worried briefly about what Brand might be up to next and called in Bob Essex. The two men entered into a deedy conversation until the telephone rang and the now familiar voice of Superintendent Josh Buller barked triumphantly into his ears.

'We've got him. Gilchrist. Heathrow.'

## CHAPTER TWENTY

As he climbed the stairs to his flat Brand heard his telephone ringing with that nervous irritation which a phone can transmit by some kind of telepathy when it's about to cut off a call to an unanswered number.

He quickened his pace, fumbled for his keys and opened the front door, knowing as he did so that the ringing would stop the moment he reached for the receiver. It did. If it's important, they'll call again, he assured himself, but it didn't assuage the certainty that he'd missed out on something vital by a split second.

The evening was suddenly uncomfortably warm for the time of year. No tremor of sea breeze ruffled the functional, mole-coloured curtains. The airless atmosphere gave the furnishings and fixtures a dead look. Dull, dull, thought Brand. For the first time he saw his living-room as others might see it. A typical home for a retired bachelor with no interest in his surroundings beyond a modicum of comfort and amenities that worked.

He mentally reminded himself that he really should do something about redecorating and refurnishing the place. Then he poured himself a Guinness, shed his jacket and slumped in the armchair that had been part of his habitat for as long as he could remember. That could do with re-covering, too.

But his mind wasn't really on the niceties of interior decoration. It simply delayed the problem he knew he would be wrestling with long into the night.

The past few days had sped by, carrying him along on their own momentum, shooting sights, scenes, impressions at him with machine-gun rapidity. It was the right climate for swift judgements. But swift judgements weren't Brand's line. There'd been disturbingly little time to think. Two people were dead. One man was strongly suspected. The evidence against Russ Gilchrist was overwhelming. Why couldn't he accept it like everyone else?

He closed his eyes, not from weariness—though he was desperately weary—but as if he were hoping that by so doing he might blot out all that had happened.

Four days ago he'd been pottering around, spinning out unimportant daily tasks to make them seem necessary, trying to convince himself that he'd earned the peace and pace of his retirement and therefore he was enjoying it. And perhaps he had been, more than he realized, then.

Four days ago he'd cherished an illusion about Charlotte Saint-Clair. A silly, old man's illusion which mistook the fantasies she'd projected in the cinema of his youth for reality. It was the reality of Charlotte, as he'd learned about it from Sam Ackerman, Joanna Saint-Clair, Gloria Beesley, Joe Gannis, which had been more shattering even than her murder. The face, that wonderfully arresting face, had been just a mask, a disguise for a shallow, conniving woman who had tainted so many lives and certainly ruined one.

For a few moments he allowed himself the

luxury of wallowing in his own disillusionment. Although he'd never met her, she'd been a part of his life and she'd destroyed that part as surely as she'd destroyed the woman who'd once been her best friend, Leila Starr.

Then he felt a rising anger replacing the morbid self-pity. A strong sense of purpose began to course through his veins, giving his tired limbs a fresh vitality.

'She's not going to destroy another life. Not if I can help it,' he said out loud. He levered himself clumsily out of the chair, took out a pad of paper and a pen from a drawer which he laid neatly on the table, lit his pipe and then sat bolt upright on a kitchen stool staring at the blank pages facing him.

Rapidly he began to write, dividing the text into two columns headed 'For' and 'Against'. Within an hour he had a list of names with comments separated into the dual sections. After one item—'J.St-C's brakes, car accident'—he doodled several question-marks, then triumphantly scratched them out. When he'd finished writing, he studied the pages intently, altering here, correcting there, linking one name to others with looping arrows. Then he stood up, stretched his arms and looked at the scrawled paper with a glow of satisfaction.

At the end of the text two names in capitals were heavily underlined. ARTIE NOLAN and EMILY JACKSON.

'That's it!' He placed his hands palms together in front of his mouth, admiring his handiwork. 'That is *it!*'

But there was no time to be wasted. The longer he delayed, the greater the threat to Joanna Saint-Clair. He dialled her number at her aunt's cottage. The engaged tone partially alleviated his fears, until it persisted every time he tried to phone again.

His car was parked in front of the flats. Within thirty minutes he could be there. Before leaving he put in a call to the station. One thing his experience had taught him over the past few days was to err on the side of caution. He didn't intend to be clobbered twice.

Waller wasn't available, his sergeant, Bob Essex, told Brand. He'd been called to London by Superintendent Buller. He started to say 'by the way, Mr Brand...' but Brand cut him short. He spoke hurriedly.

'Be sure Waller gets the message,' he urged.

'But Mr Brand...' Essex tried again. But the line was dead. Brand was already out of the door and on his way.

★     ★     ★

As he walked up the drive to the house where Charlotte Saint-Clair met her death, after parking his car in the lane outside, Brand noticed with relief that a light was burning in an upper room and the hall. The blaze from the uncurtained windows shed an eerie glow on the flower-beds, draining them of colour. As he knocked on the front door the sound seemed to echo through the house. It felt like several minutes but was probably no more than one before Joanna Saint-Clair opened the door.

She was wearing a flimsy pink negligée over a nightgown and her hair hung loosely, languorously, round her shoulders.

She gazed at him through those keen eyes, momentarily surprised, then yawned sleepily. 'Mr Brand! I can't think . . . I was asleep.'

'Your phone didn't answer.'

'I left it off the hook. Wanted to get a good night's sleep.'

'What about the people from the village? They were supposed to be staying with you.'

'I sent them away. There didn't seem much point. The police assured me Russ wouldn't be likely to attempt anything.'

She'd assumed he knew about her accident with the car.

'Miss Saint-Clair, I must speak to you. It's very urgent.'

'About Russ?'

'No, not Gilchrist.'

She seemed taken aback, but recovered herself quickly. 'But it was you who warned me about Russ.'

Brand raised his hand. 'I know, I know. I was

wrong.'

'Mr Brand, I really am very tired. A bit sore, still, too.' She deliberately touched an angry bruise on her forearm as if to draw his attention to it. 'Can't it wait until morning? I'd rather you didn't . . .'

'Miss Saint-Clair. Joanna. There's no time. Tomorrow may be too late.'

She allowed herself a small, mocking smile. The kind of smile she was very good at. 'You mean I'm in danger from somebody else now?'

'If you want to put it like that. Yes.'

The smile slowly retreated leaving a thin, hard line around her lips.

'Mr Brand, to be frank, I've had enough of you. You barged in on me when you had no authority. I took you into my confidence. You advised me about Russ. Now you say Russ is innocent. I'd rather leave it to the police. *They* seem to know what they're doing.'

She made as if to shut the door, but Brand wedged his shoe firmly in the aperture. 'I *have* to speak to you. And if you don't speak to me, Inspector Waller . . .'

'Let him in, Jo. Persistence like this deserves some reward.'

The voice behind her came from the stairway. A cool, collected voice, sure of itself. It was a voice with no fear in it.

'I can't . . .' she began.

'Yes, you can. You must.'

Limply her hand dropped to her side as Brand pushed the door wide open.

He was conscious of that faint aroma of sandalwood which he remembered smelling before he'd been attacked in this very house.

Standing on the stairs, an easy, threatening grin on his pleasant face, was John Arthur. His feet were bare and a bathrobe was loosely belted round his waist. He pulled the collar of the robe to cover his chest. But not before Brand had caught a glimpse of a heavy gold chain with a strange, lettered clasp round his neck.

'Clever, Mr Brand,' said John Arthur admiringly. 'But just a little too clever, I think. Well, don't just stand there. Come in.' He nodded to Joanna Saint-Clair.

As Brand turned, he found himself looking into the barrel of the Colt automatic which she was holding steadily in her hand.

# CHAPTER TWENTY-ONE

'You look a little surprised, Mr Brand. Not quite what you'd expected?'

John Arthur was lounging confidently on Charlotte Saint-Clair's delicate Victorian *chaise-longue*. He was making no attempt now to disguise the heavy gold chain which swung provocatively from his neck, his fingers playing

215

easily with the amethyst clasp, constantly tracing the damning letters 'L' and 'C'. But Brand wasn't deceived by his apparent air of lazy comfort. He sensed the coiled spring of tension within the man, realizing that if he made a move Arthur would be one jump ahead of him.

Joanna Saint-Clair was standing stiffly by the closed sitting-room door. She'd pocketed the automatic, but her hand was flexed, ready for action. Although she kept looking steadily at Brand, he felt that mentally she was trying to avert her eyes as if—unlike Arthur—she was not relishing the situation that had been forced on her.

They'd directed Brand to the upright chair by the fireplace, cornering him from any possible escape. Short of bounding through the locked french windows like Superman, he was trapped.

'No comment, Mr Brand?' Arthur prodded him.

The first shock of realizing that Joanna Saint-Clair was implicated with Arthur had abated. There was no time now to examine his reaction to that. For the moment the only priority was survival. He hadn't the slightest doubt that Arthur intended to kill him. But the man was a showman, too. He clearly enjoyed the suspense, the build-up to the climax, the euphoric pleasure of seeing his audience sweat a little before the end. Indulging that pleasure, reasoned Brand, was his only chance, a slim one, of getting out of the house alive.

He reached into his pocket and instantly Joanna Saint-Clair produced the gun, her index finger on the trigger, pointing it at him accurately. 'Just my pipe,' explained Brand, holding his faithful briar in one hand so that both could see it clearly and his pouch of St Bruno in the other. 'You wouldn't deny a condemned man a last smoke.'

John Arthur shook his head admiringly. 'Such cool! Is that what they teach you in the police force? Under stress, always keep your cool. Best way to wear down the opposition. Such a pity it's wasted on us. I've waited too long to be beaten by a washed-up, over-age copper. And you know, Mr Brand, you really do show your age.'

'How come?' said Brand, trying to sound disinterested.

'You're not like the younger chaps. No sentiment in them. I suspect you're the sort of man who's always looking for damsels in distress to rescue. I suppose in your courtly, old-fashioned way you reckoned if Jo didn't need to be rescued from Gilchrist because she was too close to the truth, then it followed she needed to be rescued from me. Bad miscalculation! As you can see, the damsel isn't distressed at all.'

Without taking his eyes off Brand he turned his head towards Joanna.

217

'Perhaps you're right,' conceded Brand. 'You're a pretty good actress, Miss Saint-Clair. Almost as good as your aunt. Maybe you took lessons from her. But, you know, she had a little trick that was sometimes irritating. When she knew she'd made an effect in a certain scene, she'd just overdo it, embellish it. You picked up that trick when you faked your car accident. I admit I didn't see it until just now. Which was my mistake. I should have remembered how efficiently you fixed the starter motor on your car when it kicked out. It wouldn't have been difficult to tamper with your own brakes and then make sure you weren't in any great danger when they failed. I suppose it was worth it. One more nail in poor old Russ Gilchrist's coffin.'

'It was worth it,' she said coldly.

'What does surprise me is that he—' Brand indicated John Arthur—'would allow you to take that risk. After all, it could have gone horribly wrong.'

For an instant Brand felt a *frisson* of doubt passing between Joanna and Arthur. But just as suddenly it was dispelled.

'Divide and conquer, Mr Brand,' said Arthur softly. 'You've been seeing too many TV cop shows. They're not like life. You should know that.'

'I do,' Brand replied guardedly. 'But do you? My impression of show business people is that very often they can't tell the difference. For instance, why milk the excitement? Why don't you kill me right now? You are going to kill me, aren't you?'

'I'm afraid, Mr Brand, we have to.' Arthur sighed in mock sorrow. 'You're the man who knows too much.'

'And what do you intend to do with my corpse?' Brand knew he was taking a dangerous chance, but he was betting on Arthur's sense of the theatrical. 'Let me guess. You'll dump me somewhere near that cottage Gilchrist rented. And the gun? Of course, it's Gilchrist's gun. The one you or Miss Saint-Clair took away from him before convincing him that he was wanted by the police and urging him to disappear. The one that killed Sam Ackerman. The gun's a poser. I wouldn't risk it near the body. Too obvious. Maybe plant it somewhere that Gilchrist frequented. I'm sure you've plans for the gun. That is, of course, if Gilchrist hasn't already been apprehended.'

'But he hasn't, has he?' said Arthur. 'We know where he is, safely, lying low.'

No, damn it, thought Brand, they hadn't caught Gilchrist. At least, they hadn't when last he saw Waller which was only a few hours before.

'And when Gilchrist is miraculously produced, he'll deny everything. How will you deal with that?'

'Simple, Mr Brand, Joanna, as you said, is a

very good actress. She had the best teacher. The police already know how scared she was of Russ because she suspected he might have murdered her aunt. You were very helpful there. Played right into our hands. We really owe you and your meddling an awful lot. That's why we're having this nice little chat. You deserve to know the whole story—before you die, that is.'

'What makes you think I came here alone? Perhaps the police are outside the house now.' God, if only they were, thought Brand.

'Good try, Mr Brand. But I think we know you pretty well by now. You're a loner. It's your failing. Why else did you come here the other night on your own to snoop around? Sorry about that lump on your head, by the way.'

Brand fingered the sore spot on the back of his head. His pipe, that act of bravado, lay unlit in his lap. 'My error,' he agreed. 'But yours too, I think. Stupid thing to overlook, wasn't it? The two pieces of incriminating evidence—Leila Starr's chain and the letter her sister Emily sent to Charlotte on Leila's death. You were taking a chance, weren't you, stealing in that night?'

'Not really.' John Arthur seemed unshakable. He had an answer for everything. 'The police weren't much interested in the house, so it appeared, after they'd removed Charlotte's body. It was easy to slip in.'

'Miss Saint-Clair could have done it in broad daylight. After all, it was legally her house.'

Brand paused. 'No, I suppose not. You couldn't take that chance. Once you'd realized the chain and letter were still in the drawer of Charlotte Saint-Clair's bureau you had to get hold of them immediately. Just in case some nosey copper— like me—decided to examine the house and its contents more thoroughly.'

'Right again, Mr Brand. You really are doing well. Ten out of ten. And, as it happened, it turned out to our advantage, didn't it? You get thumped by an unknown assailant. The chain and note disappear—except they've only your word that they existed. Who but the elusive Mr Gilchrist would have been responsible?'

Brand looked at the man in amazement. It wasn't the cold-bloodedness, the arrogance of him, that were appalling. It was the matter-of-fact way in which he discussed another man's conviction for crimes he hadn't committed.

'How on earth do you think you're going to get away with this? Both of you.' He shot a disgusted glance at Joanna Saint-Clair who returned it coolly. 'And patient investigation about you, Arthur, would turn up the same evidence I and Sam Ackerman discovered.'

'But why should the police bother to dig that deep, look any further? They'll have the man they want, the man they're scouring the country for, the man whose gun killed Ackerman, who had no alibi for the times when the murders were committed. Most of all, he had the motive.

221

Charlotte destroyed his career—or so he believed. And anyone who knew him would testify he was the kind of half crazy character who'd be capable of killing her to get even.' John Arthur spoke equably, ordering his arguments, as if to a retarded child who hadn't quite grasped the simple facts of life.

'You *are* a monster!'

It was an involuntary expression of horror that escaped before Brand could contain it. He hadn't wanted his anger to explode. It would just add to John Arthur's pleasure. But it had been wrenched out of him against his will.

'What do you know about monsters, Mr Brand?' Joanna Saint-Clair countered fiercely. 'Charlotte was a monster and millions of people worshipped her. Being monstrous pays off.'

John Arthur observed the two of them calmly, almost clinically, as though they were acting out a scene in a plot of his devising. Which, in a sense, Brand realized, they were.

'Temper, Jo!' Arthur warned in the professional tone of a producer giving stage directions. 'What I'm really curious about is how did you catch on to me?' he said, dismissing Joanna and turning his attention to Brand.

'The same way Sam Ackerman did, I imagine, Mr Arthur. Except I don't think your name is John Arthur, is it? Maybe Arthur Jackson? Your mother, Leila Starr's, maiden name was Jackson and your father was Artie

222

Nolan. John Arthur was a serviceable substitute—changed by deed poll, I suppose. It kept reminding you of who you were, but it was just different enough to disguise your identity from any prying busybodies. Now it's my turn to be curious. How could you keep that hate alive for so many years? Twenty, thirty years?'

'Longer than that, Mr Brand. A lifetime.' There was a dry, far-away resonance in Arthur's voice which seemed to echo through the corridors of a tormented past. The crisp professionalism of a moment ago had been squeezed out of it, like the juice from a lemon, at Brand's mention of his mother's name.

'Actually it's Arnold Jackson. Mother never liked the names Arthur or Artie. Otherwise you're quite correct,' Arthur continued. 'And you're right, I had to hold on to the memory of who I was. Hate, Mr Brand, hate is the great, consuming passion. Love is transitory. But you can feed on hate. It nourishes you. When you're sick, hard up, down and out, hate sustains you. In the household where I was brought up it was the eleventh commandment. Other children learn to say the Lord's Prayer, honour their parents, do unto others. All I ever remember from the time I was able to take in anything was being taught to hate Charlotte Saint-Clair.'

'Who taught you that? Leila?' Brand interrupted softly, not wanting to force the man back into the present.

'Leila!' John Arthur chuckled to himself. 'Poor Leila. By the time I was really aware of her, she was incapable of formulating anything as positive as hate. Have you ever watched someone you love disintegrate, piece by piece? Can you imagine seeing a glowing, adorable human being decline into a dissolute hag, not suddenly, but slowly, day by day, month by month, a little worse? And you knew there was nothing you could do to help, because she'd given up. It was I who found her when she committed suicide. And I was glad. Not because she was dead—in every way but in the physical sense she'd died years before when Hollywood abandoned her. When Charlotte Saint-Clair "killed" her. I was glad because she didn't have to drag out her left-over life any longer. And I was glad because I could get on with what I had to do.'

'Was it her sister, Emily Jackson, who kept the hate alive?'

Arthur nodded. 'She never let me forget. She recited the sins of Charlotte Saint-Clair like a catechism. I remember the pleasure she took in sending that note and Leila's chain to Charlotte. "That's the beginning," she said to me, "now it's up to you." When Emily died, I was at college in Boston. I never finished the course. I left America, changed my name, although no one was interested in Leila Starr any more, bummed around Europe for a bit and then I discovered I had a talent for writing. I didn't do badly. I settled in England. One play got good notices but it never transferred to the West End. Then I did bits and pieces for television, built up quite a reputation. For a while I thought maybe I could exorcize the ghost of Charlotte Saint-Clair. But there are some ghosts that can't be exorcized, not when you've lived with them as long as I had.'

There was a sense of release in the way the words came tumbling out of Arthur's memory. Perhaps, thought Brand, this is the first time he's been able to utter them. He looked across at Joanna Saint-Clair. She was staring mesmerized at Arthur as if she were seeing him for the first time. Maybe she was. The real Arnold Jackson had kept himself hidden, disguised, for so long. Brand doubted whether he'd told a fraction of the story he was telling now to Joanna before. Just enough to enlist her sympathy, her help, to nourish her own grievance against Charlotte Saint-Clair, to make them allies in a common cause.

Arthur seemed unaware of them, threading his way through a sordid confession that perhaps, in his deranged mind, might give him absolution for the crimes he'd committed.

'When Sam approached me to provide an outline for *Wild Fortune* it just seemed a nice, secure source of income. And then he told me they'd got Charlotte Saint-Clair to star in it. I remember he said the name with a sort of awe. The great lady. Dame Charlotte Saint-Clair. No longer in her prime. But still a *coup* for the series. I thought this was my chance. I could write out my hatred of her through the character I created for her, Chelsea Fortune.'

'But that wasn't enough, was it?' said Brand.

The man looked up abruptly. The veil of memory lifted from his eyes. Almost visibly, the obsessed, tormented boy Arnold Jackson reverted back into the ruthless *persona* of John Arthur. Playtime over, he seemed to be saying to Brand.

'No, it wasn't enough. I created a loathsome woman. But the public adored her. The more evil she was in the series, the more they loved her for it, the more successful she became. So, you see, Mr Brand, I had to kill her, hadn't I? There was no other way. And it was so uncomplicated. She was actually glad to see me that night. She thought the show had gone so well. She congratulated me. But mostly she was congratulating herself. At first I don't think she realized what was happening when I stood behind her and started tightening the chain round her neck. She laughed. Then as I twisted the chain and told her who I really was I felt the fear flooding through her body,' Arthur's fingers were tugging feverishly at the chain round his own neck, reliving the moment of Charlotte's death. 'She knew why she died, Mr

Brand. That was the beauty of it, she knew. I'm sorry about Sam. But he shouldn't have delved into the past, just like you're doing.'

'And Joanna? Was it easy to persuade Joanna to be an accessory to the murder of her aunt?' Brand said as if she weren't there.

'Jo and I are in love.' The word tripped off John Arthur's tongue with none of the conviction he brought to 'hate'. 'I saw the way Charlotte treated her. Jo deserved her reward, her inheritance for those years of miserable servitude. Charlotte was the sort of woman who'd live to receive the Queen's telegram on her hundredth birthday. We just hurried the dying process up a little.' He spoke flatly, as if reciting the boring trivia of another episode of *Wild Fortune* which didn't have to be convincing, merely entertaining.

From the way she was looking at him, half pleading, half stricken, Brand realized that the change in Arthur, from the fanaticism of his memories to the cool callousness of his attitude to the reality of their joint crime, hadn't been lost on Joanna Saint-Clair. Deliberately, with no undue haste, he rose from his chair and moved towards her. 'Don't,' she said feebly.

'And you, Joanna!' Brand coaxed her quietly. 'John Arthur had his reasons. But what about yours? Were they just as solid? Were they worth two people's lives? Are they worth the imprisonment, for life probably, of a man who trusted you?'

'Jo, don't let him con you. He's good at that.' The menace in John Arthur's voice was underlaid with a trace of uncertainty.

She looked nervously from Arthur to Brand. 'My reasons were just as good as John's,' she said with an attempt to retrieve her old composure.

'Were they?' Brand moved almost imperceptibly nearer to her. 'You can't even call him by his real name. You don't even know him. You don't think he did this for love of you, do you? You don't think he even cares about the money you'll inherit? He did it out of revenge. A revenge in which you have no part at all.'

She edged away from him, though the gun was still clasped firmly in her hand, pointed somewhere in the region of Brand's heart. She gripped it as if it were a lifeline, perhaps the only comfort left to her.

'You're doing very well,' Brand went on. 'But this is only the beginning. How are you going to feel during the long trial of Russ Gilchrist when you have to get up in the witness-box and lie and lie and lie? How are you going to cope when you wake up at four o'clock in the morning and all the fears and guilts crowd in and you can't wipe them out with sleeping pills? Well, there's always John Arthur, isn't there? He'll look after you. Maybe he will. But maybe he won't. You'll be tied together for the rest of your lives by a shared guilty secret. And perhaps one day he'll decide he doesn't want to go on paying his dues to you. After all, he's committed two murders. Another won't make much difference. Only it won't look like murder. It'll be a neat, convincing accident—just like the sort of thing he dreams up for his television shows.'

Her lips were trembling and tears were trickling down her cheeks, but she stubbornly persisted: 'It's not like that. We love each other. He said so.'

'I'm sure he did, many times. Words, Joanna! Words are his business. And murder. Now he wants you to murder me. Because then there's no way that you can escape. He wants you to pull that trigger. Look at him. He's begging you. Kill, kill, kill, Joanna!'

Brand knew he'd worn down what was left of her resolution. He also knew that John Arthur was on his feet, behind him, ready, waiting. But neither of them could risk an ill-judged move. A gun in the hand of a nervous human being wasn't choosey about its targets.

In the distance he heard the sound of tyres crunching to a halt on the gravel lane outside the house. Brand couldn't allow himself the comfort of hoping it might be Waller. But the faint noise deflected Joanna Saint-Clair's attention momentarily. It was long enough. As Brand reached quickly for the gun, he felt John Arthur's strong arms strapping themselves round his body like a vice. He grasped Joanna's hand, edging it out of lethal range. There was a loud report and Brand felt a searing pain as if his shoulder was on fire.

Slumping to the ground, he saw John Arthur wrench the gun from Joanna's hand. He rolled out of range, wincing as his shoulder brushed the thickly carpeted floor, a trace of blood scarred its deep pile. He closed his eyes as John Arthur stood over him, aiming to kill.

He was only dimly aware that the front door was being battered open and that the room was being invaded. Too late, too late, he thought. Then he heard the noise of a scuffle, the crash of a chair, shouts. He waited still for the *coup de grâce* and then realized it wasn't going to happen. When he opened his eyes Sergeant Bob Essex and a constable were holding John Arthur. Another constable was gripping Joanna Saint-Clair's arm.

Brand looked up at John Arthur. But he wasn't John Arthur any more. He was Arnold Jackson with the wounded eyes of a young boy who had carried the burden of vengeance for too long.

'Why?' whispered Brand. 'Why didn't you pull the trigger?'

John Arthur just shook his head in a puzzled fashion. 'I underestimated you.' It was no answer. Perhaps there was none, except in the deep recesses of Arthur's subconscious where the demons of guilt had finally asserted themselves.

John Waller was propping Brand against the *chaise-longue*. Idly, Brand noticed, it too was stained with his blood. He attempted a weak smile. 'What took you so long?' But he was breathing so heavily that he doubted whether Waller heard.

## CHAPTER TWENTY-TWO

'Congratulations! You're quite a hero.'

Ralph Brand was propped up in a hospital bed with his arm in a sling and his shoulder feeling as if an army of elephants had trodden on it, when John Waller arrived with a clutch of newspapers which he dumped on the prim white and blue counterpane.

Brand picked up the most garish tabloid. There was an elderly photograph of himself taken when he was in his prime, looking smug and self-sufficient and a pillar of the police force. He winced at the report underneath and tossed it aside.

'Co-star billing with Charlotte Saint-Clair. Who'd have thought it,' said Waller.

'The stuff that dreams are made of—or nightmares,' Brand murmured.

'Hurt?' Waller indicated his shoulder.

'Yes.'

'Well, at least, we're not having a whip-round for a wreath. By the way, Buller sends his regards!'

'Big of him,' Brand acknowledged wryly.

He eased himself painfully into what he hoped would be a more comfortable position. 'There's one thing that's been puzzling me, Waller. I know I left a message at the station where I was going. But why did you think it urgent enough to follow me when Essex radioed the message to you on your way up to London?'

Waller grinned. 'You don't think you've really been doing all your investigation on your own, do you? I've kept tabs on you since you were conked on the head at the cottage the other night.'

'You mean you and Buller set me up, just like Arthur and Joanna Saint-Clair set Russ Gilchrist up?'

'I wouldn't put it quite like that.' Waller had the grace to look contrite. 'But in your quiet, stuffy old way you seemed to be getting closer to a solution than we were. So we let you get on with it, while we kept a discreet but watchful distance.'

'And almost got me killed in the process!'

'But you weren't, were you?'

'Only because ... I don't know, because of what? Maybe the psychiatrist who examines John Arthur will find out.'

'Don't follow you, Ralph. When we burst in he just realized there was nothing to be gained by killing you.'

'I doubt it. He wasn't—isn't—a simple man. For years he'd been living two lives. Who knows when that burden became too heavy to bear. I was just lucky. Have you seen Gilchrist?'

'Not yet. Buller's got him. He'd been shacking up in a flat of a friend who was abroad. Fortunately for him—and for you—he panicked and decided to make a run for it. You know, Ralph, I've never been able to understand the gullibility of the human race. He believed every word Joanna Saint-Clair told him.'

'Why shouldn't he? He trusted her. Poor devil. Perhaps she was the only person in the world he did trust. What'll happen to him?'

'Nothing much. Except owning a firearm without a licence.'

'And Joanna Saint-Clair?'

'Accessory before and after. The press will have a field day. Haven't had such a good juicy trial since the Yorkshire Ripper. Well, I'd better be off, just thought I'd see you were comfortable. I've kept the reporters away. But they'll probably start pestering you as soon as you're fit.'

'Not if I can help it. As soon as I'm fit I'm taking a holiday. Maybe Salzburg. I always wanted to see where they shot *The Sound of Music*.'

Waller chuckled. 'That figures! Well, if you hadn't been such a movie fan maybe we never would have got to the bottom of Charlotte Saint-Clair's murder.'

'Oh yes you would. It would just have taken a little longer.'

A starchy young nurse poked her head round the door. 'Time, gentlemen, please,' she said primly.

'You don't suppose I could have my pipe and pouch?' said Brand.

The nurse sighed disapprovingly. 'We don't encourage smoking among the patients,' she replied.

'Can't do me much harm now.'

'Well, just don't make a fug in the room. Matron doesn't like it.'

She dug the pipe and frayed pouch out of his jacket pocket and handed them to him with some distaste.

Waller turned and waved at the door. 'Try not to get into any more trouble. Not yet, anyway.'

'What, here? Fat chance.'

The nurse sniffed.

When she'd shushed Waller out of the room, Brand switched on the radio and, handicapped as he was, took his time lighting his pipe. The news was all about the sensational developments in the case of Charlotte Saint-Clair's and Sam Ackerman's murders.

He switched it off, irritated by the cold, blaring voice of the newscaster, droning on about a fantasy creature named Chelsea Fortune as if she were flesh and blood, the receptacle of the life that had been Charlotte Saint-Clair's.

Maybe in the quiet of the hospital room he could conjure up the memory of the legendary star he'd loved and forget the rest.

Photoset, printed and bound in Great Britain by
REDWOOD BURN LIMITED, Trowbridge, Wiltshire